THE STRANGER RETURNS

MARK McGUNEGILL

Primix Publishing
11620 Wilshire Blvd
Suite 900, West Wilshire Center, Los Angeles, CA, 90025
www.primixpublishing.com
Phone: 1-800-538-5788

Published by Primix Publishing: 05/23/2024

ISBN: 979-8-89194-185-4(sc)
ISBN: 979-8-89194-186-1(e)

Library of Congress Control Number: 2024911254

CONTENTS

CHAPTER 1

THE QUESTION OF
TIME TRAVEL

I pondered over it many times while lying on my cot staring into the dim light of my sleeping compartment. It was not a new question or one that I had to work out myself. Albert Einstein developed his Theory of Special Relativity more than a century ago. But I became the first human guinea pig on whom its affects would be tested. It's hard to visualize it, unless you have a mind like Einstein's. Simply put, the theory states that the relative or perceived passage of time would be different between an observer on Earth and one traveling through space at very high speeds. For the space traveler, time would pass more slowly than for people on Earth. Upon his return to Earth, the space traveler would experience a perceived acceleration through time, perhaps months for years or even days for years. It would depend on many factors such as acceleration, top speed, distance traveled and proximity to strong gravity fields. There were enough people willing to take the risks to find the answers to those questions, even if they never lived to see it.

The months of isolation might have driven most people mad. But for the most part, I prefer being alone with my thoughts to the company of others. Almost every moment that passes I find myself regretting not having spent more time with my wife and daughter before the accident which snatched them away from me so suddenly. As a test pilot, I was away for weeks at a time. But I could have made more of the time we had together. I was crushed and broken in spirit. The Air Force gave me a few months leave of absence and eventually I ended up in the Reserves, still maintaining my rank of Major. After that I threw myself back into my work with a vengeance, volunteering for the most exotic and dangerous assignments. It was tough to keep up the façade of a well-adjusted human being, but it was necessary to keep my psychological profile clean so I could continue working. In fact, I was only two months from my silver leaf when I was launched into space.

The late twenties and earlier thirties were a renaissance of space exploration for the United States. But by 2034, the year I was launched, economic troubles were spreading around the world like a virus. Economies and currencies were nearing the breaking point and governments were losing the means and the will to continue further ventures in space. For this reason, the launch of this experimental spacecraft and its mission was kept top secret. But I did not need or want the publicity or fanfare. I did not even care if I would be remembered. Since I was a boy, I felt like a loner and a stranger in the world, always looking beyond what is, trying to imagine what could be.

I am Major Joshua McNeal, United States Air Force Reserve. My goal in volunteering for the mission was not to commit suicide or to entomb myself in a 20 billion dollar coffin hurling through deep space. But rather I wanted to live to see a different and better world.

Even theoretical physics suggests that traveling backwards in time is impossible. Once events have passed, they can never be revisited. And I am content to see the past sink into the deep sea of forgetfulness. But for better or for worse, the future holds endless possibilities. The one certainty is that there will be change. But will I live to see the change? Have I traveled far enough and fast enough to really make a difference? Will I arrive in a new world as a hero, or will I arrive back in my old world as a laughing stock and a failure? These questions have filled my brain more and more as I come to the closing leg of my long journey. There are no instruments that can tell me how much time has passed on Earth. There is no way of knowing the effects of the time differential until I actually land on Earth and see it for myself. No mortal can know the future until it becomes the present.

The second approach toward the sun would be the most dangerous because of the relatively close proximity the ship would come toward it. My speed through space would at that point be so great that it could not be calculated by instruments. Why? Because the relative speed of the ship moving toward or away from celestial bodies has to figure in those bodies own movements through space as well as any time differential affect that may greatly accelerate those movements. This was indeed an experiment, wherein the exact outcome could not even be postulated. My speed upon leaving the sun's orbit would at that time be so great, that the 93 million mile gap between the sun and the Earth could be covered in less than ten hours according to computer estimate. But most of that time would be spent decelerating therefore the time to final approach would be stretched to four or five days.

Nine months have I spent traveling through space many times faster and farther than any human has ever gone. I spent nine months monitoring volatile nuclear engines, eating, sleeping, exercising, watching movies, playing games on the computer and just thinking. For nine months my life was spent in a 800 cubic foot womb awaiting to be born again into a strange new world. My long journey was coming to an end. The computer alerted me that the engines had slowed to the point where conventional navigation was possible again. The Earth was visible only as a small blue dot bearing three, one, zero degrees off the nose of the spacecraft. For all my misgivings about the human race, something deep inside me was happy to see the Earth again and to finally come home.

As for the question of time travel, I placed that in the back of my mind for the time being. My questions would all soon be answered if and when I could reach Edwards Air Force Base in California or some other flight control center in the United States. But the bigger challenge would be to pilot the ship through the Earth's atmosphere and land it safely. I got into my flight suit and secured myself in the pilot's seat.

CHAPTER 2
NO WELCOME

The lights and displays in the cockpit all lit up like a Christmas tree. The Earth at that point was about the size of a tennis ball outside the forward window. It looked like a blue and white jewel hanging in space. To me it was the most beautiful planet in the solar system. That opinion I am sure was mixed with a lot of emotion, after seeing most of the other neighboring worlds. Every single one of them is strange, lifeless and deadly. But I was not home yet. Many things could go wrong before I would touch down on the dry lake bed at Edwards. Or looking at it the other way, many things had to go just right for me to land safely at my destination. I was still traveling very fast. The ship was slowing, but was it enough? Was I on course? I had to trust the computer at that point.

I knew the time had come to talk to the computer and have it radio in. I hesitated for a moment. Who would answer? What would they tell me about the world I was approaching? How different would it be, or would it be different at all? I had an anxious lump in my throat. But I could not put it off any longer. I spoke.

"Computer, contact flight control."

"Contacting Space Flight Control, MCC - Houston." The computer answered.

Some months earlier, I selected a seductive female voice for the computer, just to make things a little more interesting. My playful repartee of course was not reciprocated by the computer, but my imagination was enough. I finally got used to her, so I left it on that setting.

"No response, Major." The computer reported after several minutes.

"Keep trying, sweetheart." I said casually, but getting a bit concerned.

I waited nervously for several more minutes with no response. The Earth was gradually growing larger in the window.

"Try Edwards Air Force Base Flight Tracking Center." I ordered in all seriousness.

"Edwards Air Force Base is not tracking by radar and not responding." The computer answered back.

"Try Vandenberg or Nellis." I said sharply as I monitored my approach.

"No response, Major." She said after a few more minutes.

At that point, I was feeling desperate. Had there been a nuclear war? Was I returning to a devastated world? I wanted to hear a real human voice. Re-entry and landing would be extremely difficult at best, even with the help of the computer. The plan was to make two orbits before landing. The first was to be far at about 350 miles altitude and the second one close at about 150 miles altitude. But I needed ground tracking to help guide me in. The retro engines were not nuclear powered, but conventional rocket engines. They had been firing intermittently for the last several million miles. I could only pray that I would have enough fuel left to slow my approach to Earth. I decided to tell the computer to stop transmitting and start monitoring.

"Computer, scan ITU region 2 in the VHF and UHF bandwidths."

I was at that time, close enough to Earth to clearly see the major continents and polar ice caps. While the computer was scanning for transmissions, I was asking her about my speed and the narrow angle of orbital approach I had to hit very shortly. Even if the world was devastated, I had to land the ship, by myself if necessary. Then she spoke again.

"Scanning radio communications on 330 Megahertz."

"Lock on and patch me in." I said with excitement and relief.

I reached over and switched on the microphone.

"This is United States Air Force spacecraft EX-501 calling any tracking station. Over."

There was no immediate response, so I repeated the call. Then I heard a voice mixed with intermittent static, come in over the speaker. He did not sound like an American, he sounded more European, but I didn't care. At least he spoke English.

"Did you say United States Air Force? Over."

"That's affirmative. United States Air Force. Who am I speaking to? Over.

"You have reached WSA Communications Center in Brussels. And there are no spacecraft near Earth or any scheduled to return, especially from the United States. Over."

"What happened? Why can't I reach any tracking center in the United States? Over."

"Who is this?" The man on the radio became more guarded.

I started to answer, but thought better about it. This mission was top secret and was probably not even revealed to other American agencies, much less foreign ones. But still I wanted to extract as much information from the guy as I could while telling him as little as possible.

"I have been away for a long time. What about the United States?

"There is no more United States. There hasn't been for almost twenty years. It's been absorbed into the North American League together with several other countries."

"My God." I whispered to myself.

"Can you please tell me sir, what year is it?"

"What year is it? Where did you launch from?

"I'm returning from a several month long mission exploring the outer Solar System. Can you please tell me the date and year?

"It is March 14ᵗʰ, NE 12."

"What is NE 12?"

"It is the twelfth year of the New Era."

"New Era? What's that?"

"Where have you been? It was when all the nations finally came together to form ten Leagues or Federations, all under common leadership. It was the end of different economies, the end of poverty and the end of war."

"Two hundred nations consolidated into ten? And what about the former way of calculating the year?"

"That was based on ancient mythology. But we still allow people to refer to it. Some would say that it is the year 2096."

"Thank you."

"You are using a secure government channel. We need to know who you are and where you are."

At that point, I switched off the radio, the radar and the transponder. It was clear that they had no knowledge of me or my mission. My own country was not even a country anymore. Obviously, there would be no ticker tape parade for Major McNeal. The beautiful blue Earth filled the left half of the forward window. With the help of my lovely electronic companion, I was able get into position for my first orbit.

As I gazed down at the Earth, I marveled at the fact that the planet never seems to change. People change, societies change, but the good old Earth keeps spinning and looking the same. But I was still concerned about my speed. My first orbit was completed in less than three hours. The retro engines were burning on and off for about half the time. When I pulled the ship in closer for my second orbit, my speed naturally increased, much like an ice skater spinning on one blade can spin faster if she pulls her arms and leg in closer to her body. I was at 150 miles altitude when my retro engines were firing at full throttle constantly. My rocket fuel was getting low. The computer was guiding me toward a landing at Edwards.

But what if there were no Edwards, or Vandenberg or any other place controlled by an American government? I could not let myself or this ship fall into the hands of some strange, foreign government. My mind could not fully fathom what had happened to the world. But my imagination ran wild. I decided to ditch the ship in the ocean off the California coast. It would be extremely dangerous, but if I survived, at least I might have freedom of movement for a while. When I was about 400 miles northwest of the Hawaiian Islands on compass bearing 057 degrees, I instructed the computer to adjust my speed and angle of descent to land the ship in the ocean about half a mile off the California coast. She protested. The ship was not designed for a water landing. As it was, I would skip like a flat stone thrown across a pond, possibly for a mile or more. If I hit any kind of sizable wave, the ship would crack up and that would be the end. She was right of course. It was dangerous and impossible to accurately judge, even for her. But I kept overriding her warnings.

"It's nice to know you're concerned about your Daddy."

Once again I had to let my mind escape the seriousness of my situation. She did not respond. I was scared. As I descended to about 30,000 feet, I could see nothing but ocean all around me. The retro engines were cutting back because the atmosphere itself was slowing my air speed. Since I did not want to send out any signal, I kept my radar off and just kept scanning the horizon for any recognizable land form. This was what the old guys called flying by the seat of your pants. But I was still doing better than Mach 2 and it could be another hour or so before I sighted land. She did not like what I was doing at all. But she expressed this by offering endless alternatives, all of which I had to lovingly reject. Finally, I decided to just take the stick and fly the ship myself.

"You've been wonderful darling; we'll do it again some time."

I switched her off. I flew the ship using only sight, feel and judgment. But judgment was very difficult when you have no radar or radio to guide you and no target in sight. The balance between air speed and rate of descend could be very delicate. Too fast and the ship would plow into one of the coastal cliffs. Too slow and the ship would just drop into the sea. I engaged the crash harness and held the ship steady.

Calculating just by dead reckoning I must be getting close. So I slowed to Mach 1 and descended to 20,000 feet. And soon I saw in the distance, a group of islands about 150 miles out. Could those be the Channel Islands? They had to be. If so, then I should soon see the California coast. In a few minutes, there it was! The California coastline! I had to slow and descend quickly. My plan was to fly in south of those islands. As I got closer, I definitely recognized them as the Channel Islands. They look like the same dry shrub hills that permeate most of Southern California except these are sticking out in the ocean. Strangely, I did not notice any boats or ships around which surprised me since these were popular destinations for boaters.

The coast was coming up fast. I just had to slow; the descent would take care of itself. I was below 10,000 feet as I was passing the islands on my left.

"Flaps down, nose up, throttle back!"

I would often think out loud in stressful situations. The water was speeding by under me. I noticed white caps which suggested a choppy sea, just what I did not need. At 5,000 feet, my landing gear was still retracted giving me warning lights. I had to ignore them. No landing gear would be deployed, I was about to become a speed boat. The computer may have been right. I thought to myself. She was just looking out for me. What in hell did I think I was doing? 400 miles per hour was as slow as I could get the ship to go and still keep it in the air. Approaching to within three miles of shore, at 1,000 feet altitude, I held on tight.

The ship belly flopped on the water and skipped back up into the air. I yelled in agony. It felt like I got hit by a truck. The ship was still moving forward at a high speed but my control over it was at an end. The second hit on the water occurred only five seconds later, it was less severe than the first, but my body was already rattled. I was just praying that the ship would not flip over. Finally, the ship made a third and a fourth hit in rapid succession, glided on the water a short distance, then came to rest floating upright.

After I pulled myself together, I realized that the ship would not be afloat for long. Water was leaking in from various points in the fuselage and steam was spreading throughout the compartments from water coming in contact with hot engine parts. The cockpit hatch was half submerged. But there was an emergency escape hatch on top. I quickly released my harness as I saw water rushing into the cabin. The emergency hatch was equipped with breakaway bolts and an explosive charge to blow it free. Every muscle and organ in my body was in pain. I was wading knee deep in cold water while breathing hot steam. I saw the flashing red light and the push button below, which had a clear plastic cover over it. When I pulled back the cover, I punched the button with my fist and the hatch blew off revealing the open sky. I struggled to climb up and when I was half way through, I noticed the small compartment next to the hatch which contained a life raft. The cover of this compartment was flush with the outer hull except for a recessed hand hole containing a handle which when twisted and pulled hard, the cover would open. I pulled out the tightly compacted raft, pulled the cord and threw it in the water. It completely inflated in ten seconds.

With all the determination I could muster, I pulled myself through the hatch and stood on top of the ship. She was sinking right under me, so I jumped into the water and swam for the raft. If my flight suit were not buoyant, I would have drowned for sure because every movement of my arms and legs was torture. Still I had to make it to the raft and climb in before stiffness set in. I grabbed a handhold on the side and pulled it toward me. First, my right arm went over, then my left arm and head. I pulled with all my strength and managed to raise my right leg up into the raft. One more desperate pull turned me over on my back, face up in the raft.

The raft was equipped with a small telescoping aluminum oar, several packets of freeze dried rations and a quart of water. But I could not deal with any of that at the moment. I was unable to move at all for several minutes as I lay on my back seeing only the sky above. I do not know exactly how long it was before I was able to lift my head up to look over the side. When I did, I could no longer see the ship. It was, I presumed, at the bottom of the ocean. The shore was a mile and a half or two miles away. I could not tell whether the tide was carrying me in or pulling me farther out to sea. But I still could not get my stiff, aching body to sit up and start rowing. I just lay back down and trusted the wind and the waves to work for me, for I could do no more.

At some point, my body just shut down and I fell asleep. This was evident because I was awakened by another jolt. The raft stopped suddenly when it hit the sand on the beach. It looked like late afternoon and the surf was high. But as I was looking around at a deserted beach, another wave came crashing in behind me, pushing me forward and filling the raft with water. I grabbed my rations and moved up the beach, not even considering what should be done with the raft.

My legs ached as I trudged through the sand carrying only the small waterproof bag which contained my provisions. Thankfully, my flight suit was insulated and non-porous so I did not remain cold and wet. At last I was able to take a good look around. Everything was very strange, not at all as I remembered it. Not only was the beach and higher ground above void of any people or vehicles, but it looked as though it had been completely devastated. Much of what were the coastal hills and cliffs were eroded down onto what used to be streets and buildings, even down to the beach. I saw what looked like great mud slides which covered much of the town and stripped the land of most of the vegetation. But what town was it? Oxnard? Port Hueneme? I could not be sure. The buildings that I saw on higher ground were abandoned and in ruins. My curiosity carried me forward. This kind of destruction did not appear to be the result of bombs, nuclear or otherwise. Things were flattened, washed away or buried in mud. All indications suggest that this was the result of a massive earthquake or tsunami wave or both.

Looking at the giant piles of silt, they appeared to be completely dry. They even had a few sparse plants and weeds growing on them.

Those made me think that this did not happen recently. It may have been like this for years. But why was no attempt made to rebuild or even clean up the mess? Maybe I would find out, maybe not. As the sun was setting, I walked still farther inland. Most of the roads were not passable. It was like walking over a barren wilderness rather than the streets of lively beach town. Just before dark I spotted the shell of a concrete building. The walls were still standing and most of the roof was intact, but it was completely empty. I spent the night in that building huddled in a corner on a cold concrete floor.

CHAPTER 3

THE OUTLANDS

As soon as I saw the first light of day coming through the wall openings, I picked myself up and crawled out of the same lower window that I entered through the night before. The doorways were blocked by mounds of dirt and debris. When I got outside, I saw a beautiful blue sky, billowy white clouds and a cool ocean breeze blowing. It was just like my fondest memories of the beach. But instead of strolling through the shops and sidewalk cafes, there was nothing but desolation all around. It was fairly evident what had happened, although I could not tell if this was the result of a single great cataclysm or a series of natural disasters. What was not clear was the reason for abandoning it in this condition. Why was there no effort to rebuild? I kept asking myself. How far down the coast did the damage go? I wondered. Some of the most valuable real estate on the planet was laid waste and abandoned. It was incomprehensible.

My body still ached, but at least I was able to walk and move about as I needed to. I was hungry, but I decided to make my rations last as long as I possibly could, not knowing when or where I might find food. Nothing was recognizable. But I decided to walk inland to try and find the Coast Highway if it was still visible. I knew that it would take days to walk the length of Malibu, Santa Monica and then into Los Angeles. If I kept the ocean always on my right, that would keep me going in the right direction. It would also be necessary for me to search out stores or any place that I might find provisions and a change of clothes. Another thought crossed my mind. Why were there no people visible anywhere in this region? Was it because most of the population had died? Or was it because this was a quarantine area, off limits and patrolled by air or some kind of surveillance? Was I being watched even now? I wondered. These concerns were also on my mind, especially when walking in open areas.

The rough and irregular terrain took a lot of energy to cover. Eventually I learned to recognize when I was over a road or highway because the silt flow and debris ran flatter and straighter over the wider roadways. Even though I was trying to conserve my meager rations, I was constantly on the look-out for a source to replenish them. I explored several abandoned buildings, hoping to tap into their water supply, but the water had long since been cut off. In my travels, I could not even find any of the channels that run storm water to the sea. I assumed that they had been broken up or completely filled in with silt.

As I continued inland a little farther I noticed a substantial concrete overpass that was mostly intact. I walked toward it. I could see that it supported what used to be a substantial highway. After crawling over mounds of dirt and debris which filled the street below it, I finally got under it to search for any identifying markings on the bridge. At last I saw stenciled on the concrete Pacific Coast Highway. That was it! The highway I was looking for. I knew that this road, as cracked, buckled and covered with dirt as it was, would be a direct route to Santa Monica.

But I also knew that as I traveled south and east on the Coast Highway, that it would move closer to the beach and therefore subject to more extensive damage. Still, I had no choice. The only other option would be to go farther inland over the rough, steep hills. And that would be much slower and more difficult. I climbed up onto the highway and found it to be severely damaged, but it had less debris covering it than the streets of the town below. I figured that I could make good time on this road, at least for the next several miles. There were fewer structures along this route and therefore less debris to be an impediment. I walked vigorously for the rest of the day. As the sun was going down, I looked for some kind of shelter to rest in for the night. I was in an undeveloped area where there were no structures or remnants of structures. The steep sandstone cliffs were right next to the highway. They had many crevasses and shallow caves from years of erosion. I decided to crawl into one of the caves, but it was not even large enough to spread out and lie down in. Once again I was grateful for my insulated flight suit because a cold and steady ocean breeze was blowing in my direction all night.

The morning light did not come too soon for me. I could not remember spending a more uncomfortable night. As I sat up and prepared to crawl out of the cave, I thought I heard a muffled roaring sound approaching and getting louder. It was not a familiar sound. It was not the wind or the surf, but more mechanical, like some kind of an engine. I nestled back into the cave and poked my head out only enough to see the highway. The sound grew closer and louder. And then I saw it. They were two fast moving vehicles that appeared to be flying only a few feet above the highway. The vehicles reminded me of motorcycles because they each had two wheels which could be used for traveling on smooth road surfaces. These vehicles were equipped with some kind of jets which could be engaged to hop or fly over uneven terrain. Unlike motorcycles of my time, these were completely enclosed in a streamline body which covered all internal parts. The riders appeared to be police or military of some kind. They were in all black helmets, visors and body armor. The vehicles were all white except for a large governmental seal on each side, which I could not read or make out.

I waited until the vehicles were well down the road and out of sight before crawling out of the cave. My fears were confirmed. These regions were being patrolled and watched. Since I have seen no other people except police, it was apparent that the whole area was off limits and the police were being employed to catch any trespassers. I certainly had no desire to be stopped and possibly arrested. So as I continued my journey I would avoid staying out in the open too long so I could jump for cover if I heard something coming. But there was always the possibility that the area was being monitored by cameras or by aircraft although I had not seen any. Still I could not figure out why they were so concerned about this wasteland. How far did this devastation spread? Where was the population? I redoubled my efforts to get to Santa Monica which I thought would provide a smoother and more direct route into Los Angeles, if it still existed. As evening approached, I found a wide crevasse in the dirt, one of many in the area made by water erosion. It was big enough to lie down in so I would be below the surface of the ground. Thankfully, the soil was dry and stable. But still I would spend another not so pleasant night.

Malibu, home to the rich and famous lay before me at about midday. The Coast Highway was no longer discernable as it approached the beach. The hills of Malibu looked as though they had been liquefied and poured down into the sea. Large pieces of buildings and what used to be multi-million dollar homes were poking up out of the dirt in every orientation imaginable. It was a bizarre landscape of total destruction. It would be a difficult passage, but still easier than trying to traverse the hills and canyons inland. At least I had plenty of cover if another patrol should come by.

My rations and especially my water were running low. I had to replenish them, but where? I had no choice but to continue. As I walked, I looked up at the sky and noticed that there was an overcast developing which in a way made me feel a little more secure. The harsh sunlight seems to make everything stand out more. Also, I was hoping that it might rain so at least I could replenish my water supply. My flight suit was getting cumbersome to walk in. I wanted to shed it so badly, but underneath it I was wearing only what amounted to long underwear. But I was alive and still free. I knew where I was and where I was going even though it looked like everyone's worst nightmare had come true.

As I was walking, I was thinking only of putting as many miles behind me as quickly as possible. Then I heard a familiar sound in the distance. It was the smooth roar of the flying motorcycles speeding toward me. I ran down to the beach and took cover behind a large section of a roof gable protruding up out of the sand. They sped by quickly from behind as before. But this time, they slowed and stopped a little way up ahead. There were two of them as before, but this time one of them turned right and flew back out toward the beach. I quickly dug some sand away with my hands and crawled inside the gable. The vehicle made a long and wide circle passing over me very closely. It circled back to rejoin the other one and then they both sped away. I lay in that cramped space for what seemed like a very long time. What made him stop and take a second look? I wondered. Maybe he saw my footprints. Whatever it was, it made me realize just how vulnerable I was while walking out in the open.

After that, I was in no particular hurry to proceed. I crawled out but rested close to the gable. Perhaps I had to re-think my idea of not traveling at night. After all, it may be more dangerous walking, but I would not be seen as easily and that is what it was all about. I lay there for a while looking up at the sky which was growing darker. It looked like it may rain at any time. If it rained, the gable would provide reasonable shelter, so I stayed close.

That afternoon, it started to rain, lightly at first, then strong and steady. The gable was still attached to another section of roof which formed a valley. The valley had a sheet metal flashing on it and over the broken end, water poured out like a faucet. I filled my water bottle and filled my mouth with as much water as I could drink. The thought of possible radioactive contamination did cross my mind. But dehydration would have been a more immediate problem. I crawled back under the gable to wait out the worst of the storm.

The rain stopped sometime during the night. I rested, but I was not able to sleep. My plan was to get up and get going again, walking at night. The clouds were separating with the stars visible in between. It was a half-moon that night which allowed enough light to proceed. I walked with renewed confidence with the cover of darkness. Looking ahead, I could see no artificial lights, only a darkly silhouetted landscape. But in the distance, far to the east, I could see a glow on the clouds as if from a city.

I saw no other patrols for the rest of the night. When I noticed the sky getting lighter ahead of me, I knew that dawn was near. As I got further into Malibu, I discovered many larger, commercial buildings which were not completely torn apart. They were severely damaged and partially buried, but there were many places of shelter where I could stop and rest. I came upon the remains of a three story office building of some kind. The first floor was a total mess of dirt and rotting carpet and furniture. But as I walked up the stairs to the second and third floors, I saw several offices that suffered relatively slight damage. Even many of the windows were still intact. I lay down on the clean dry carpet of an empty third floor office, wishing with all my heart that I could go somewhere and get a cup of hot coffee and a toasted bagel. But I settled for a few hours of rest.

Around noon I woke up from my best rest since I landed. But anxiety and curiosity would not allow me to prolong it. As I progressed into east Malibu, I noticed that the effects of the enormous tsunami wave were diminishing. The hills were not eroded away so deeply and the silt flow was becoming shallower. But what did not diminish were the effects of a massive earthquake, or perhaps a series of earthquakes that shook many buildings right off their foundations. When I arrived at the approximate border between Malibu and Santa Monica, I saw to my horror, a large building of about 25 stories that fell right into the road. The debris of the building was so high and wide that it stretched from the hill all the way down into the water. It was the most complete roadblock imaginable with no passage over, around or through.

My only option was to double back and climb up and over the hill on the inland side. So that is what I did even though climbing in a space flight suit was extremely difficult. I wanted to get over the hill and back onto the road before dark. On the summit of the hill, I could see ahead what looked like an abandoned city in shambles, but with little or no effects from the giant tsunami. It was a disaster area, but much more easily passable on foot. And I was optimistic about finding some provisions and clothing somewhere in that abandoned city.

The road past the fallen building was still buckled and broken, but less covered with silt except for one section by the pier where part of the hillside and road above had completely collapsed down onto it. So I walked down by the sand of this once very popular beach, but on that day, there was not a soul in sight. I did not go out onto the pier to reminisce about old times. In my college days, I would take a girl out there for a date a couple of times. One of those girls was a cute but quiet little blonde named Kathy, who would later become my wife. But the pier had none of its former glory or attraction as with everything else it seemed.

As I traveled south and east along the Coast Highway, it became just one of the many major streets that ran through the city. Many buildings were partially or completely shaken apart with mounds of debris filling the streets. But other buildings seemed to fare better with only some broken windows and trim, but structurally still sound. There were still no people visible anywhere although the density of the city afforded many hiding places. I wondered if I was being watched through any one of the many dark windows that surrounded me. And I knew the very real possibility of more flying motorcycle patrols. They could post up anywhere out of plain sight and roll up onto anyone who showed themselves, and I had no way of knowing what kind of electronic detection devices they may have. I decided to walk along the side streets and alleys that paralleled the main streets. My destination was the downtown area.

By that time, the ocean was miles behind me and the hills were nowhere near. I was in a mostly residential area, but I could see the larger commercial buildings through the broken and abandoned houses. I found myself walking down the street of what was once an older but more upscale neighborhood. One particular house on that street seemed to tempt me to investigate further. It was a larger home of Spanish style architecture which was mostly intact except for some stucco cracks and some boarded up windows. The solid Mahogany front door was securely locked. Broken windows or sliding glass doors were typically covered with a sheet composite material similar to plywood. This particular house had a partial second story which was perhaps an add on room addition containing a bedroom and bathroom. I noticed one unbroken sash window on the second floor which was partially open. This window was easily accessible from the first story roof, and the roof was easily accessible from the limb of a large, mature Elm tree which was next to the house. I climbed the tree just like I was ten years old again, despite my cumbersome flight suit. A short walk up the roof, breaking a few tiles as I went, soon brought me to the open window. I pushed it open all the way and stepped in.

The room I found myself in was a large bedroom which looked like it had been used as an office. There was a large Cherry wood desk near the window but nothing much else in the desk or in the room. I looked in the attached closet and bathroom, but both were empty and void of anything useful. The only light available was that which came through the open window. While in the bathroom, I saw myself in the cracked mirror over the sink. I looked derelict and unshaven with wildly messed hair and several days' growth of facial hair. Disgusted by the sight of myself, I quickly exited the bathroom and went into the short hallway which led downstairs. The house was quite dark because all but a couple of small windows were boarded up.

The larger pieces of furniture were left, but most of the smaller and personal items were gone. I rummaged through every drawer and cabinet I could find. There was nothing found of any use. Neither the kitchen nor pantry contained anything edible. I started to get frustrated and angry. They did not even leave me a shaving razor or comb. So I decided to just make myself at home for a while. I flopped down on their nice big sofa, put my feet up and took a nap for a few hours.

When I finally woke up, it was pitch dark in the house. I estimated that it may have been eight or nine o'clock in the evening, but I had no way of knowing for sure. There was a laundry room window that I remembered which was not boarded up and large enough to crawl out of, but as I groped through the darkness to find it, I discovered that it was screwed closed. So I slowly and carefully found my way back upstairs and out the window that I came through. The moon gave enough light to see to make my way down the roof and then down the big sturdy Elm tree and down to the ground.

I was starting to come to the conclusion that the police did not patrol at night. Perhaps it was just wishful thinking on my part, but I was not seeing or hearing them at night, probably because finding anyone in these regions at night would be nearly impossible. So again, under the cover of darkness, I proceeded toward the more commercial areas of town. My rations were almost gone and I was getting hungry and anxious. Still, as I walked, I would keep an ear out for that familiar low pitched roar.

The darkness was a mixed blessing. I felt reasonably secure about evading the police patrols, but neither could I see most opportunities that might be out there for me to exploit. After about two hours of walking, I came to a boulevard lined with stores, restaurants and other businesses, most of which were destroyed or boarded up. I began to reason that the demolished buildings, which were open, may have been looted long ago. But the buildings that were still standing and boarded up may still have some useful items in them if I could get in.

There was a building which used to be a food market. It was smaller than a supermarket but larger than a neighborhood grocery store. The building was boarded up, but was much more intact than many of the others. I walked around the building to see if I could detect any gap or loose screws in the sheeting in which I could insert a piece of steel to pry it off or bust it open. Finally, I found an opportunity. It was one of the many sheets that covered the front glass windows. One panel near the end was a bit out of alignment with the window frame and several of the screws on one edge were not making contact with anything solid. I was able to pull it out far enough to get my hand in, but pulling as hard as I could was not enough. I needed leverage.

There were several debris piles in the area. So I walked around looking for something I could use to pry the board off. At last I found a large piece of angle iron that was about seven feet long and looked as if it was used for a temporary sign. I rushed back to the market with my tool and immediately went to work. The stiff metal piece slid right in and with only a slight tug, I was able to break the screws out one by one until the heavy sheet crashed to the ground. I used the long metal piece to break out the large remaining pieces of broken glass. With each stroke I looked around anxiously because I was making considerable noise.

It was a deep and dark cavern that I stepped into. What I could see of the market near the opening were shelves and display cases that did contain some items however few and sparse they were and much of it was strewn all over the floor. I had to take a few minutes to allow my eyes to adjust to the increasing darkness as I made my way deeper into the store. The place smelled musty and dusty and I was sure that it must have been rodent and insect infested. My only goal for the rest of the night was to find a place to hold up inside until dawn. I needed some light to examine the food to tell if it was fit to eat. Since I could not see what kind of creatures might be in here with me, I was reluctant to sit or lie down anywhere. So I spent about an hour just slowly walking around inside.

Then suddenly a bright red line of light burst into the dark store from outside the opening. I quickly crouched down behind the end of a shelving unit. I stayed still and silent. The light was a laser beam which scanned the entire store from side to side and from floor to ceiling. It was a shock to me because there was no sound at all, just suddenly a bright narrow beam of light. I did not hear the motorcycles or even anyone approaching on foot, and I was on the alert for them. After a few scans back and forth, the light went off and again without a single sound.

I waited silently and still for the sounds of police entering the store, the shining of flashlights or searchlights and calling out. But after several minutes there was still no sound at all, no voices, no footsteps, no engines, nothing. I moved slowly toward the opening, trying to stay in the shadows. Nothing was visible but the empty street outside. Could it have been just a routine search? But I was not sure of by whom or by what. I moved back to the rear of the store and sat in an empty produce shelf. It was as comfortable a spot as possible given the circumstances. I sat there just watching and thinking while dozing off only occasionally.

When the morning light poured through the opening, I could see the store and what remained of its contents. There was dust and spider webs all about with a few cockroaches and spiders scurrying around in the open. I did not see any rodents at the time, but there was certainly evidence of them. Every cardboard box and bag containing food was eaten through and its contents ravaged and spoiled. Out of curiosity, I examined some of the boxes of crackers and cereal to try and see an expiration date printed on them. That date would tell me, within a few months, when the disaster happened. Then I spotted a box of cereal with only a small mouse hole eaten through it. It had a blank white box on the back with the words next to it *SELL BY:* and a date stamp 03-15-2075. That told me that the great earthquake must have happened in late 2074 or early 2075. So my goal became to find canned or jarred food that could still be good after more than twenty years.

It appeared that food cans were being made out of a durable organic plastic instead of metal. And to my relief, they could be opened without any kind of tool. The shelves looked like they were pilfered through shortly after the quake, then at some point, the authorities came through to take everyone away and sealed up the buildings as best they could. I managed to extract a full meal from the remnants of the store and washed it all down with an undamaged bottle of mountain spring water.

I slowly walked toward the opening and peeked out into the bright daylight. Without a sign of anyone or anything moving around, I walked out and continued my search, carrying my long piece of angle iron with me. The street that I was on was only about a block from the main downtown boulevard. My goal was the larger stores and buildings along the downtown strip. There was a lot of broken glass, debris and trash in the streets. But the big buildings were only boarded up on the street level. I thought that if I could break into a department store, I could find clothes and other useful items.

As I walked, I once again felt as if I were being watched. I thought I detected something moving in my peripheral vision. But when I turned, I really could not see anything definite. It seemed like a slight blurry spot flying or circling around me, but nothing solid, nothing I could define. I thought for sure that my eyes or brain were playing tricks on me; anxiety combined with insufficient sleep can do that. After stopping for over a minute, carefully examining my surroundings, I decided to just move on.

Then suddenly, just as I was about to go up an alley, I heard a loud voice that sounded like it came from a loudspeaker. I turned and there was a small grey elliptical sphere about three feet in diameter, hovering in the air only a few feet from me. It startled me, because I did not hear it approach.

"Stop! Do not move!" The amplified electronic voice commanded.

It was a drone but with no visible rotor blades. The motive power was all internal and extremely quiet. The only appendage on the solid grey shape was a small glass dome on the underside, which I presumed contained a camera and or scanner.

"Present your identification." The drone demanded.

My military I.D. was at the bottom of the ocean and somehow I did not think that would help me even if I had it. I just stood there looking at it, wondering if it was being controlled remotely by a human being, or if it were a fully functional computer program,

"Present your government I.D. card for scanning." It again demanded.

I clenched tightly to the piece of angle iron in my hand as the drone repeated the command in Spanish, French, Arabic, and four different Asian languages.

"This is a restricted area. Citizens are prohibited. Stay where you are and wait for officers."

I turned my back on it while looking around trying to figure out what to do.

"Stay where you are and wait for officers." It repeated.

Almost out of pure instinct, I grabbed the angle iron at one end with both hands like a baseball bat. Then I turned and swung at the drone. The iron bar easily cut through the light material of the outer skin. Its flight control and equilibrium had been severely damaged. It was flying erratically and running into buildings while still repeating the command to wait for officers. I also got an insight as to why I never saw it coming. The outer skin was like a high resolution LCD screen which projected the image of whatever was behind it. Effectively, it was an almost flawless camouflage device. But the damage I caused was making the image flash on and off, intermittently revealing its shape and betraying its secret. But I had no time to ponder over it. I had to make a run for it before those officers arrived.

The alley was narrow and filled with piles of assorted materials. There was only enough room for a person to pass on foot, but that was enough. I ran when I could, then watched and hid. The buildings provided good cover, so I tried to stay close to them. As I ran and watched, I kept listening for the dull roar of the flying motorcycles. Perhaps they were hold up around the next corner, waiting to pounce as soon as they saw me. I came to the end of the alley, and in front of me was a wide open street. The buildings on the other side were bigger and suffered more damage. Large pieces of wreckage fell in front of some of the entrances. I gambled that perhaps I could pry through the debris enough to crawl inside. Staying just behind the outer corner, I peeked down the street both ways and up in the air. It was clear, so I ran as fast as I could to the large building across the street in which a large structural canopy had collapsed over the entrance.

There was a gap of just under one foot between the fallen wreckage and one of the entry doors which had not been boarded up. I inserted the angle iron and leaned into it with all my strength. The iron bar was bending, but it had widened the opening just enough for me to squeeze through. I was in. As I quietly laid the iron down, I heard the familiar sound of the police vehicles. I could only see a small section of the street through the narrow opening, but it sounded like at least two of the vehicles were circling above the block that I came from. A minute later I heard and saw through the gap, two other vehicles on the street, rolling like conventional motorcycles. I moved back away from the gap and the light that was coming through it. My heart was pounding as I stood motionless in the store until I heard no more sounds outside.

It was a good size department store which from what I could see in the dim light, was not as heavily picked through as it could have been. Shelves and clothing racks were knocked over and strewn about. Parts of the suspended ceiling had fallen down. And the banks of escalators stood still and silent but were largely unobstructed. The sunlight leaking through some small gaps and a few second story windows was the only light in the place and even after my eyes adjusted, it was barely enough. So while it was still daylight, I decided to go shopping.

When I finally stumbled upon the men's department, I really did not have the luxury of shopping as I would have since the whole place was in such disarray. All I wanted was a good durable shirt and a pair of pants that would fit me. I removed my flight suit and tried on several since I could not even read the labels. At last I found suitable clothes and light boots, which were dark in color so that I would not stand out like I did in my white flight suit. The items I found were comfortable and fit well although style wise they would not have been my first choice, but the price was right. I stuffed my flight suit under a pile of clothes on the floor so it would not be readily visible.

My next stop would be upstairs in the sporting goods department. It was a bit eerie walking up the motionless escalators and stepping on a few ceiling panels as I went. I found one of the things I was specifically looking for which was a portable light. Compact LED lights, some still in the packaging, could be found on the floor upstairs. Fortunately the compact lights still worked very well. I held one in my hand and stuffed a couple more in my pants pocket. It had to be used sparingly and briefly, not just because of the old batteries, but any light which could be seen outside through a window or break in a wall would advertise to the police that someone was in the building.

I wanted to improve and even change my appearance especially my facial hair which was in the shabby looking stage before one could call it a full beard. I found some disposable razors, shaving cream, scissors, a hair brush and a towel which I gathered up and took over to the restroom which was in the back corner of the second floor. Once inside, I was confident in turning on my light since it was a sealed room with no windows. About half of the mirror which once was mounted over the sinks and counter was still on the wall. I carefully picked up the larger broken pieces of glass and tossed them on the floor. Since I had no running water, shaving with only cream was slow and tedious. I went over to the toilet tank and removed the lid. It was still almost half full of water since it was not cracked. I dipped one end of the towel in the water and wiped off my face and dried it with the other end. After that I gave myself what I used to call a 50 cent haircut. When I was low on funds and could not afford a professional haircut, I would sometimes stand in front of a mirror and cut my own hair with a pair of scissors, pulling out strands of hair and cutting them until everything looked reasonably even.

The sun had already set by then but before I got to the escalator to go downstairs again, I noticed a distant glow shining through one of the windows facing east. As I approached the window, I could make out what appeared to be tall and fully illuminated buildings in the distance. That had to be either Century City or downtown Los Angeles itself, although the building outlines were nothing like I remembered them, still it was understandable that there would be change after 62 years. One thing was sure; it was a lighted, living city, not a dark and abandoned one. My survival depended on finding food, water and people that could help me. Still, I needed to be cautious and to blend in with the population until I could figure it all out. But there was no remaining in these desolate regions for me. I walked out of the store into the darkness and headed east.

I tried to avoid the main boulevard which would have been the easiest and most direct route only because I did not want to be spotted by another drone. The drones might have been completely invisible at night if they had perfected the technology of matching the lighting as well as the background on their projection shell. So the only thing that I could do would be to make it hard for them to detect me, since I could not see them. I kept close to the big buildings, or what remained of them and stayed in the shadows. All through the night I walked in a generally eastward direction, using the moon as a guide. At some point in the very early morning hours, I saw an enormous chain link fence which was more than twenty feet in height and ran in a north to south direction for as far as I could see. It was supported not by poles, but by steel towers which housed bright lights shining down on both sides of the fence. This fence seemed to mark the end of the abandoned city, for on the other side of it was a wide highway with relatively few vehicles moving very fast on it. Beyond the highway was a sea of ultra-modern looking apartment buildings and residences which looked very much alike. There were even the tracks of an elevated monorail train which looked as if it ran from the residential area all the way to the downtown area. The centerpiece of the downtown complex was a massive wide and tall cylindrical building all lit internally and shining in the dark like a diamond.

My curiosity compelled me toward the fence to get a better look, but I stopped and drew back. I could not allow myself to be under those bright lights and God knows how many cameras as well. I retreated back into the dark ruins of the abandoned city, trying to think of a way through the fence and across the highway. As I walked down a dark sidewalk, I noticed a manhole cover over a large storm water catch basin. I put my fingers in the small grab holes on the rim of the cover and I pulled. But I could not lift it. Desperately, I searched for something to pry it off with. Then I saw just a few yards away, a cinder block wall partially collapsed with some of its steel reinforcing bars sticking out. I raced over to it and grabbed one of those bars, racking it back and forth until it finally broke off. The bar was just over a foot long and small enough to fit in the hole. I successfully pried the cover off and aimed my light down into the structure. There was a set of rungs leading down from the hole about twenty feet to what looked like a large pipe running eastward to westward. I turned off the light and climbed into the hole, and then I replaced the heavy steel cover back over me. Now that I was inside the pitch dark structure, I turned my light back on and slowly climbed down to the pipe.

CHAPTER 4

THE CITY

The concrete reinforced pipe was about four feet in diameter. I knew that it must have been well over 100 years old and had been out of service for some time since no water was flowing through it. There was damp silt and debris along the bottom. I had to walk through it crouched down which made my neck and back sore after about 50 yards.

During my rest stops, I would shine my bright, compact light down the pipe ahead of me. It was straight and unobstructed as far as I could see. Hope and curiosity drove me forward. I needed that pipe to keep going, under the fence, under the highway and right into the outskirts of the city. But I also had to find another catch basin or manhole that was not sealed up or covered.

I estimated that I would have to travel at least half of a mile from the structure that I entered to get to the other side of the highway. After that, I had no idea how far the next structure would be where I could climb back out. The air inside the pipe was dank and musty.

But the pipe kept on going straight toward the city, for which I was grateful.

The thought kept racing through my mind that they may have sealed it off at the other end. But for what purpose? Why would anyone want to escape into the desolated outlands? I raced ahead as fast as I could; given the awkward position I was forced to take on. My immediate motive was either to prove or disprove my fears. After about 45 minutes, I reckoned that I was somewhere beneath the highway. I figured that after another 100 yards or so, the very next structure would be the one to take, if there was one.

After another half hour of walking with only brief rests, I saw that the pipe just continued on as before. The next structure was not visible, but I would not see it until I was almost in it. I knew that I must have easily cleared the highway. So all I wanted to see was another catch basin to climb out through.

Twenty more minutes passed. I found myself breathing heavily, not sure whether it was from anxiety or the bad air, or both. So I rested and tried to stay calm. I focused my light to a bright, narrow beam and aimed it straight down the middle of the pipe. It ended! I was looking at a concrete wall about 20 yards ahead with no continuation of the pipe. From that distance, I could not tell if it terminated in a structure. I crept slowly forward, shining my light ahead as I went. The rim of the pipe would cast a shadow on the wall if there was any separation between them. But I could not be certain.

At last I was within just a few feet from where the pipe ended. I saw the rounded shadows moving around on the wall. To my relief, I saw that it was a small access structure. When I looked around the edge of the pipe, I saw steel rungs which led up to a manhole.

The structure was not much more than just a square, vertical pipe leading up to the surface. I put the light in my mouth and climbed up to the manhole. When I pushed on the steel cover, it would not budge. I pushed harder and pounded it with my fist, but it would not move. I did see daylight through two small grab holes on the rim. That told me that it was not covered over, but it may not have been opened for years.

In desperation, I decided to attempt some awkward gymnastics. I grabbed the rung tightly and walked my feet up above me so that I was hanging upside down. While biting down on the light, I placed my left foot next to the hole. I reared back my right leg, aimed it at the center of the steel cover and gave it a hard thrust. It loosened slightly, but did not come off. My hands were starting to hurt from bearing all of the weight and force. If I slipped, I would fall head first fifteen feet to the concrete bottom.

I held tight and gave it another hard kick. This time, it popped open and then came back down over the hole. Carefully, I maneuvered my legs back under me again and onto the rungs. I rested on the rungs for a few seconds, and then I pushed the cover as hard as I could with my arm and it flew right off the hole. The blue morning sky and the cool, fresh air gave me an immediate feeling of exhilaration.

As I climbed out of the hole, I found myself in a small utility yard with pipes and valves all exposed outside of steel buildings. All of the doors were closed and there was nobody around. I replaced the cover back over the hole and started to walk toward the large support columns of the elevated monorail train.

I approached the sidewalk that runs under the monorail and I noticed that a moving sidewalk was running parallel to the concrete one, just on the outside. There were several people walking in and around the many housing complexes. I looked down at my own clothes and the clothing that some of the other people were wearing. There seemed to be enough diversity that I figured I would blend in without too much effort.

The more I came in sight of the residents of the city, the more natural I started to feel as I walked deeper into the suburbs. People were walking past me and around me without giving me a second look. One thing I found rather strange was the fact that there were few if any personal vehicles visible. In my time, everyone had at least one car. But here it seemed that almost everyone availed themselves of some form of public transportation. There was a road on the other side of the monorail towers, but there were few vehicles on it. The vehicles that I saw were all completely enclosed streamline and quiet running. They all had different markings on them which indicated government vehicles, service vehicles or taxis. I even saw one of the flying motorcycles rolling along on its wheels.

Ahead of me about a quarter of a mile was a station for the monorail train. There were quite a few people coming in and out of the station. Loading and unloading took place on an elevated platform accessible by elevator, escalator or steps. More people were using the escalator than any of the other means. So I decided to join them and ride up to the platform, although I did not quite know what to do if they wanted money to board the train.

It felt good to be around real live people again. That was a feeling I had not known for many months. Clothing styles have changed somewhat, but people seem the same. Most of them are still preoccupied with themselves and their own business, moving straight ahead with deliberation, taking no time to notice the world around them.

When I got up to the platform, I saw people freely getting on and off of the train. There were large electronic schedule boards indicating the various station stops and the expected time of arrival for each. The boards displayed the same information in various different languages. On the train there flashed various electronic signs giving warnings and instructions using universally accepted symbols. But there was no place to pay or buy tickets or accept tickets. In fact, there was no human being working at the station or even operating the train. Everything was fully automated.

Just to be on the safe side, I asked a middle aged woman about the fare. She was about to board the train.

"You must be a stranger to the city." She said with a slight smile.

"Well, I've been away for a long time. LA has really changed." I answered.

"LA?" She asked with an expression of almost disbelief.

"You have been away for a long time. It's LG now. And there is no charge for the train anywhere within the Metroplex."

She then boarded the train and I followed, feeling a little embarrassed for my ignorance. There were display screens similar to those outside at the station hanging down from the high dome ceiling. These monitors would display the station names in the general vicinity of where the train was located at any moment, within a few miles. Most of the names were unfamiliar to me, but I did recognize a few such as Wilshire, Sunset and La Brea.

The long train consisted of three cars with flexible couplers between them covered with accordion rubber. Passengers could easily walk between cars. The train was less than half full. As the doors started to close, I found a seat near the rear of the first car, next to a window. The train smoothly and silently lifted up a few inches and then just as smoothly sped forward. I assumed that it was propelled by opposing magnetic fields, but I could not be sure.

As the train raced on, moving just above the rooftops, I could not help but marvel at the order and uniformity of the city below. The buildings were all new looking, made of a shiny, smooth almost plastic like material. The sizes and shapes did vary somewhat, but the architecture was all very similar. The roofs were all slightly domed with built-in solar panels on the southern or western exposure, depending on the orientation. Little or nothing protruded out from the roofs. The colors of the buildings ranged from white to light grey to a few light pastel colors. There were many walkways and green parkways in between and around the buildings, but very few streets. And the streets that I did see were lightly travelled by only a select few vehicles and of course, the police.

Since there was no charge for riding the train, I thought that I would just ride around the city for a while to get a good look and to see where I might want to get off. I wondered just how many other services were free since I had no money or bank cards with me. And then there was my terrible ignorance of the present state of affairs. The city was not even called Los Angeles anymore! And I felt more like a fish out of water than I ever did. But I decided to calm down and just take one step at a time.

The city looked nothing like I remembered it. Everything looked new, streamlined, clean and uniform. The old city with its eclectic assortment of houses and buildings ranging from new to more than a hundred years old was gone. The new city was not spread out as far, but it was far more efficiently compacted. Utopia? I wondered. That was yet to be seen.

The train that I was on more or less made a large circle around the city proper and all the connected districts. Shuttles would run on the narrow surface streets, taking passengers from the train stations, to the various housing complexes. The suburbs that I remembered were not recognizable and many of the names have been changed. My hometown of Glendale was completely remade. The only way that I recognized where the old city used to be was the familiar mountains and foothills, which have not changed. These hills marked the northern border of the great city. The eastern border seemed to be the San Gabriel River. It went south to about Long Beach, and on the west was the boundary that I was all too familiar with, the desolate outlands.

My curiosity became so great that I felt the need to strike up a conversation with somebody, anybody willing to answer some of my questions. There was a man travelling alone, sitting by himself in the seat right in front of me. He looked to be about my age or maybe a little younger. I decided to pretend that I was from Australia, with a fake accent to go along with it, just as a pretext to justify my terrible ignorance.

"Pardon mate. Would you know where to catch the train to downtown?" I asked, giving my best performance since my high school play. "Sure, you have to catch the transverse train at one of the stations that have the symbol next to it. See the circle with the ellipse inside of it? He pointed to a symbol that I noticed next to a couple of station stops, but I never realized what it meant.

"Oh, yes." I answered.

"Just get off at one of those stations and then you can catch the train that goes through center city." He explained.

"Thanks mate." I responded while trying to act casual.

"Say, have you been to the Tube?" He turned around again to ask me.

"No, I don't think so. What's that?"

"It's that big round building in the center city."

"You mean that big glass cylinder downtown?"

"Yeah, that's it. You have to see it while you're here. It's 60 levels. Each level is about six meters high. The center is hollow with glider bridges spanning the central core on each level. There are banks of elevators at every quadrant. The thing is half a kilometer wide, I mean diameter. And it can hold a million people."

"What is it used for?" My curiosity was re-stimulated following the man's vivid description.

"Everything. They have stores, restaurants, offices, aerial hologram theaters, anything you can think of." He continued, sounding very proud of his city's main attraction.

"I'll be sure to check that out. Thanks mate." I responded in all sincerity.

The man turned forward as we approached a transfer station. I got off the train and went one level up to board the train bound for the city center. The station stops all had different names, but I did notice the stop labelled "The Tube". That would be my destination. Looking out the window of the train, I was spellbound to see the gigantic buildings of downtown. There were tall, round double and triple towers with walking bridges connecting them at various levels. Another building was an enormous glass obelisk with a wide pyramid base. But in the center of it all, like the hub of a wheel, was the building known as "The Tube". It was a simple, perfect cylinder made of clear material like glass, and covered by a clear dome.

The train pulled up to the station right in front of the Tube. The building towered in the background like a glass mountain. Many people were getting on and off at that station. I got off and joined the masses that were losing themselves in the massive edifice.

There was a moving sidewalk bridge that went directly from the train platform into the building at the third level. Many people were with me on the inbound conveyor. Almost an equal number were on the outbound right next to it. The conveyor bridges were all covered by a clear dome. As we entered the building, it could be seen that the interior walls were also transparent and one could clearly see the people milling around in the stores on both sides of the tunnel. When we emerged out on the main concourse, it appeared that I had entered a festival of lights. Signs were not fixed and static, but bright, high resolution monitors which not only displayed the name of the establishment, but visually advertised it's products or services.

I approached the railing which overlooked the cavernous central core. Just beyond the railing was a tall and thick glass or plastic wall which circled the central core on each level. Standing behind the wall, it appeared to be just as clear glass. One could look across the expanse and see the other parts of the circular building. But that same wall was also being used to project giant video images which would go on and off at various intervals throughout the central core. The images seemed to be news items, advertisements and messages from different government agencies. I am sure that the wall I was looking through was projecting images also, but they could not be seen from behind. They could only be seen from the front by looking across the core, or from any of the bridges which spanned the core. Even the great dome, high above, projected giant images for all to see.

It was visually intoxicating like the first time I saw the Las Vegas Strip at night, but multiplied times ten. I wanted to explore, although one could spend days in this building and never see it all. The quadrants were all color coded. The floors and railings were blue, red, yellow or green and the quadrants were consistent at every level. Even the elevators, which had large, clear bubble fronts for viewing, were color coded as they travelled up and down the central core.

At various locations throughout the open concourse were informational kiosks which were four sided display screens giving visitors, location information for everything in the building. Next to these computerized kiosks were devices similar to vending machines which dispensed small, light, ear pieces that cupped over one ear. These were disposable and best of all, free. They were available in several different languages, which enabled one to hear the audio from any of the video displays that were in close proximity. One could also speak while wearing it to ask the location of any establishment in the building. The answer would come through the earpiece with the location by level, quadrant and unit.

After about a half hour of trying to absorb the overload of audio and visual stimulation, I noticed dark uniformed figures standing still at various locations not more than 50 yards apart. They were armed with an unrecognizable type of sidearm. Their uniforms, body armor, and helmets were all black. The helmets all had a dark tinted face shield pulled down so that nobody could see their faces. I suspected that these officers were more than just building security. My gut told me that they were most likely police. They looked very much like the officers that drove the flying motorcycles, which I learned were commonly called "Hoppers". From behind those face shields, they could be looking at anyone, listening to anyone or talking about anyone and nobody else would know it.

I knew that there were many people moving around in the building. But everything appeared peaceful, orderly and under control.

What was the need for so many police, here and on the roads as well? I wondered. The question was: could a utopian society and a rigid police state coexist? The answer has been written throughout history, ultimately, only if the people wanted it or allowed it. But I am just one man who wants to stay under the radar. There was nothing I was going to do about it.

My thoughts turned again to my stomach. It had been more than 24 hours since my meager rations ran out. There were eating places on almost every level, fast food as well as dine in restaurants similar to those I was familiar with. But I had neither money nor any form of payment with me. My plan was to visit a food market instead. They would be larger and I would not hold up paying customers while asking for a handout. My hope was that perhaps I could appeal to the manager for some expired food, or perhaps they would be giving out free samples.

The thought of stealing food was abhorrent to me, but if I got hungry enough, I would reluctantly leave that option open as a last resort. The closest such store was the "Garden Market" on level eight, green quadrant, unit 300. I took the red elevator up to level eight. Then I took the bridge across the open central core and over to the green quadrant. I could see the market even before I landed on the Level 8 concourse, since it was one of the largest stores on that level.

It was big, bright and full of people. Most of the shoppers were carrying large bags made from woven plastic fibers, presumably recycled. The store stocked every kind of packaged food as well as fresh produce. There were only two or three uniformed employees available to render assistance because everything else, even check out was fully automated. This was not the neighborhood market that I used to know. But then, as I approached the end of an aisle near the rear of the store, I saw an incredibly gorgeous woman standing behind a table, giving out food samples. She appeared to be a mixed race girl in her early to mid-twenties. Her assets were full, prominent and nearly perfect. The thing that made her stand out most to me was what she was wearing. It was like a one piece sleeveless jumpsuit that was open about three inches in the front from her neck to about mid torso. The material was a bright lime green, soft fabric which clung tightly to every square inch of her skin.

But as I walked closer, my interest quickly moved from her to the food samples on the table. There were meat pates and cheeses spread out on assorted crackers and flatbread. A young couple was in front of me, looking over the samples. I could see the food from behind them and my mouth was watering. When they moved on, I got up to the table. She greeted me with a big smile and a twinkle in her eye.

"Hello. How are you?"

"Oh, just fine, thanks. Everything you have here sure looks good." I answered while trying to look mainly at the food.

She smiled.

"Please feel free to sample anything that looks good to you." She said with her eyes fixed on me.

I was starting to sweat. Again, I fixed my eyes on the food and pointed to the closest sample.

"What is this?" I asked.

"Turkey and cheese pate." She answered.

I picked it up and placed it in my mouth as gracefully as I could. It was delicious. But I did not want to let on that I was half starved.

"Very good." I said calmly.

I pointed to another sample and asked about it.

"Salmon and rice. That's my favorite." She said.

I picked it up and ate it, trying to savor it, but my body would not cooperate with what my mind was trying to do. I found myself gulping it down like a hungry dog. Trying to regain my composure, I thought that I should start acting like a shopper.

"That is good. How much is that one?"

"That one is four and a half a bag." She answered.

The product came in one half kilogram bags in which one could squeeze the contents out and vacuum seal it for later. She held one up as she explained its features.

"Four and a half dollars?" I asked ignorantly, trying to sustain the conversation.

"What do you mean dollars? What's that?" She asked, truly puzzled by my question, but still smiling.

"Is it Yen, or Euros or Pesos? What form of money do you use?" I asked while trying not to be too serious.

"Coconuts." She joked.

We both laughed even as I felt a little embarrassed.

"You're funny. Credits, silly. Four and a half credits." She said with a big smile.

"Credits, yes of course, credits. I should have known."

I made her laugh. But then I looked back down at the food samples. She leaned very slightly forward.

"Is there anything else you would like to taste?"

I felt momentarily paralyzed. But I deliberately refocused my eyes and directed my hand to a chunk of white cheese on the table. I grabbed it.

"Where are you from?" She asked as I bit into the cheese.

I chewed and swallowed as quickly as I could.

"Well, I'm from right here." I answered.

"Right here?"

"Yes, from LA. I mean LG… LG, good old LG."

She laughed again.

"You're a bit strange, but interesting. Do you want to smack later?"

"I beg your pardon."

"I beg… what? What does that mean?"

"I mean I didn't understand what you just asked me. What do you mean, smack?"

"Smack, you know, sex. There are private rooms in the red quadrant, 20 credits for a half hour. Unless you think you'll need more time."

For a couple of seconds, I could not move or speak.

"Oh, well I'd like to, but I can't."

"I'm sorry." She said with a regretful look as if she thought I was claiming to be impotent.

"No, it's not that I can't. I mean I really shouldn't."

Just then, I glanced down at the plain gold wedding band that I still wore on my finger. I lifted my hand up to show her.

"Ahhh… You're a faithful husband. I think that's sweet. I remember one of my grandfathers wore a ring a lot like that. He wore it all his life."

"Well, I've got to get going. Thank you. Good Bye." I said as I was backing up to leave.

"Bye." She ended, showing no emotion.

I just wanted to get out of that uncomfortable situation anyway that I could. My libido was as healthy as any man's, but that was too much, too fast.

As I strolled along the concourse, I stopped at the closest information kiosk. The building was like a city in itself and I did a search for a branch of the public library. I needed to learn more about the world I found myself in. There was only one branch of the public library in the building. It was way up on level 55 along with several other governmental service offices and a police substation.

The elevator ride up was exhilarating. Looking down into the central core was like seeing the Grand Canyon for the first time. Level 55 was the least populated of any level I have seen. The library had few people in it and no books visible. Instead, it was a series of small booths, each with a computer terminal inside. There was no librarian or anyone working inside to assist. The monitors in each booth were voice or keyboard command and simple to activate. The research sessions were all self-directed and private, which suited me just fine. It was not difficult to find a quiet booth with nobody else nearby. When I sat down and touched the key plate in front of me, the monitor immediately popped on with a bright blue screen and the word "SEARCH" in the center. Where would I begin? I asked myself. If I wanted to find out how we got here, then I better start looking at history, even though it is a vast subject. I began my long marathon session completely oblivious to the passage of time.

The historical record was sketchy and seemed to be slanted toward a collectivist point of view. This, I was able to ascertain as much by what was left out as by the information that was recorded. In the years following my launch into space, the United States and the world found themselves in an economic crisis that threatened to bankrupt governments and collapse nations. Debt had spiraled out of control, to the point where it could no longer even be managed. The magic pills that were used earlier in the century such as printing money, buying debt, and zero interest rates, no longer worked. The servicing of debt consumed the majority of every government budget. There was no political will to control the growth of debt. Instead, there came the familiar call to raise taxes and fees. Soon, the economy which was already struggling to survive was dealt the death blow. Unemployment and inflation spread like a plague across the world.

In spite of their past failures, the Federal Government took the opportunity afforded by the crisis to exercise even more control, which included the seizure of private bank accounts, retirement accounts and many businesses. Riots and revolt broke out across the nation.

By the early forties, a revolution had begun. One of the problems with a revolution is the fact that loyalties are always divided. Family members, friends, neighbors and co-workers would find themselves on different sides of the conflict. Some of the worst betrayals and atrocities occur at these very personal levels. The bitter dissent even spread through the government and the military.

But eventually, the nation congealed into two distinct factions. The "Federalists" consisted of the entire Executive branch, most of Congress and the states and people that supported them. The Federalists were defended by all Federal law enforcement agencies and about half of the United States military forces. The other half resigned or mutinied and joined the opposition.

The "Constitutionalists" wanted to overthrow what they considered to be an unconstitutional and tyrannical government. They were supported by more than half of the states, which included Guard units or militias controlled by those states. There were also many independent militias everywhere, including Christian militias which threw their lot in with the Constitutionalists.

A long, drawn out war followed, lasting about five years. In 2046, the Federalists more or less conceded and allowed the rebellious states to form a revised constitutional government which restored rights back to the citizens and to the states. In a few years, it was back to business as usual.

In the late forties and through the fifties, America and the world picked themselves up and eventually prospered again. New discoveries in medicine and energy promised to make life better and longer for everyone. But inevitably, a generation came up who did not know the former corruption or the price that was paid to eradicate it. Europe did not experience the revolution that America did. It remained a rigidly controlled and centralized economy. America's Second Revolution seemed relatively short lived. A gradual shift in attitude took place for most Americans. A powerful central government re-emerged. But America itself was no longer powerful, economically or militarily. The records suggest that America had evolved in its attitudes and vision. But it looked to me that it had lost its vision and the love for liberty which made it great.

In 2069, the U.S. Dollar as well as many other currencies collapsed or were abolished by fiat. These were replaced by a system which was already being used in Europe. The World Bank Credit was a purely electronic system of transferring units of wealth from one account to another. It existed only in computers. No paper money or coins were minted by any government for the Credit. Credits could be exchanged for goods or services at the same rate worldwide.

Over the years, the government gradually enacted policies designed to move populations from rural and outlying areas where valuable land was being used by relatively few people, to dense urban areas where basic housing and transportation was readily available. This was done primarily by regulating and taxing people off of their large estates. Then on November 17, 2074 two massive earthquakes struck off the Southern California coast. The first one measured 9.5 on the Richter scale and was centered in the Santa Barbara Channel. This was followed six hours later by a 9.2 quake off the coast of Malibu. Both quakes were followed by tsunami waves which all but destroyed several coastal cities.

The quakes had severely damaged the city of Los Angeles and the surrounding suburbs. But the government used the disaster to advance their plan for urbanization by several years. After the living and the dead were evacuated from those hard hit outlying areas, the buildings were boarded up, and the cities fenced off and quarantined. No money was spent to rebuild or help others rebuild in those areas. Instead, a massive effort was made to remake Los Angeles into the city of the future. It was to be compact, efficient, and high tech. The new city would house all of the people who had been displaced and many more. During this process, a vote was taken to change the name from being the City of the Angels, to "La Gente," the City of the People. But people everywhere simply referred to it as LG.

The United States became progressively linked economically and politically to the European Central Government and to its neighbors to the north and south. The open borders which had been a de facto reality for many years soon became official. Then on July 4, 2076, on the 300th birthday of the nation, the Congress and the President met in a grand ceremony, with much fanfare, to sign away the sovereignty of the United States, abolish its constitution, and merge with its neighbors to form the "North American League."

I had to let several more digital books and history sites play out, even though I was sickened by what I was learning. At some point in the long session, I fell asleep in the booth as the computer ran on.

CHAPTER 5

THE FAMILY

When I finally woke up in the booth, the computer screen was silent and blank. I glanced up at the time and weather display on the wall. It indicated that I had been asleep almost four hours. Time had lost its significance to me lately. I just kept trying to follow the path of least resistance. But like a rat in a maze, I had no idea where I would end up.

This level contained mostly Government offices, so there were not as many people moving around on the concourse. Even the few police officers going in and out of the sub-station, were carrying their helmets in their hand, not really watching or patrolling this level as they did the others.

I learned in the library that every citizen was issued a Government Identification Card. This card was about half the size of the old Credit/Debit cards, but much thicker. It was made of hard, translucent plastic and had no name or markings on it. Every citizen was required to carry it with them at all times, not only for identification purposes, but for buying, selling, making or accessing payments. The card would recognize the DNA signature of its owner, and could only be activated if it were held or in physical contact with the authorized user. Some people wore it attached to a band around their wrist. There was no danger of it being used by another. If it were lost or stolen, it simply would not activate or release any information without being in physical contact with the person it was linked to. New I.D. cards could easily be obtained simply by going to any Government kiosk and letting it scan your DNA.

I was reluctant to let the machine scan me, even though I could not go on much longer in this city without an I.D. card. What kind of personal information would I have to give the computer if it could not identify me? I had no job, no bank account, no family or friends, and no identity in this world. Perhaps God would direct my steps, as my wife would say to me. But for now, I needed to walk and to think and keep my options open.

Level 32 contained a mega wholesale department and food store. It was well stocked, but surprisingly limited in the variety of items it carried. There was much less variety than were in similar stores of my time. I was however, able to fill myself up with free food samples as I strolled down the many aisles. In that particular store, thankfully I was not distracted by an aggressive, voluptuous woman which I had no time or means to deal with.

After that, I wandered back out to the concourse. I spotted an IDS machine, which stands for Identification Services. This particular machine was not near any of the police officers standing watch. I approached it reluctantly because I had no idea what would happen when I entered my name and let it scan me. There was a wide slot under the screen. I inserted my hand and a bright green light came on in and around the slot. After a few seconds, a message appeared on the screen.

NO MATCH FOUND.

The screen then popped up three question boxes, asking me to enter my name, date of birth and place of birth. One could enter the information by a touch screen keypad or by voice. When I typed the information in, the screen again displayed: NO MATCH FOUND.

I just stood there for about a minute, staring at the screen and thinking about what I should do. I must have looked pretty confused and miserable, because a lady who had just finished a transaction on a nearby machine, noticed me and stopped.

"Sir, are you alright?" She gently asked.

The woman looked to be about my age. She had plain features, but with an inner glow of warmth and kindness which I found quite attractive. A young girl of about nine or ten years old was following her. I presumed that she was her daughter. Both carried partially full shopping bags.

"Oh, I'm just a little frustrated." I answered honestly.

"Is there anything I can do to help?" She asked as she moved closer to me and the machine I was standing in front of.

"The computer can't find me." I told her in desperation.

"Were you born in the North American League?" She asked.

"I was born in the United States of America." I responded with a slight tone of defiance.

"So was I, but it is no more. What city?" She asked as she pushed through to the touch screen.

"Glendale, California."

"Glendale? I was born in Arcadia. But they're all merged into the Foothill District. You have to have been registered. I was 16 when they started mandatory registration. Okay, what is your name?"

"Joshua Samuel McNeal." I said slowly as she entered it, spelling out my last name for her.

"Nice name." She said as she glanced back at me and smiled.

"We don't hear too many biblical names much anymore."

"I suppose not in this so-called New Era."

"Yeah, I know. But I don't hold to that."

"Are you a Christian?" I asked boldly.

"Yes, I am." She replied meekly.

I smiled at her and then she turned back to the screen.

"Date of birth?"

"April 10th..." I stopped suddenly before saying the year.

"What year?" She asked as she was about to input the final bit of information.

I froze. I could not speak for a moment. Anxiety welled up in me to the point that I had to turn away. Eventually, I summoned the courage to speak to her again.

"Ma'am, I..."

"Helen, Helen Jensen. And this is my daughter, Rachel." The girl just rolled her eyes up at her mom as if she was bored by the whole thing.

That girl reminded me so much of my daughter, Audrey who was about her age when I lost her.

"Rachel, that's a nice biblical name. It's been a pleasure to meet you both. Thank you for your help and concern, but I think I need to work things out myself."

I wanted and needed help, but I did not know how to explain my dilemma.

"Do you have a family?" She asked, still expressing concern for me.

"Not anymore." I answered solemnly.

"I'm sorry. Are you a Christian?" She continued.

"My wife and daughter were. I'm still seeking. I've got a lot of questions that I need answers to."

"It's good that you're seeking. The Lord said, seek and you shall find."

"Yes, I trust that I will."

"Do you have a place to stay?"

I was a bit hesitant because I was becoming attracted to her, and I did not want to complicate my life any more than it was. On the other hand, I did need help.

"No." I answered, almost apologetically.

"Well, why don't you stay the night at our place? My husband is a computer programmer for a big electronics company. They do a lot of Government work. I'm sure that he can help you with your I.D. situation. And I'm an excellent food warmer."

When I heard that she had a husband at home, I felt much better about it. I agreed.

Our conversation on the train was more or less superficial, but it was enough to last for the short ride to a Foothill District station where we all boarded a shuttle to the housing complex where the Jensens lived. The building was similar to the thousands of housing complexes throughout the city. The construction seemed to be modular with wall and roof sections having been pre-manufactured out of a plastic like material. Sections were then brought on site and assembled into a smooth and almost seamless building.

It was a quick and quiet elevator which brought us almost to the door of their second floor apartment. Helen called her husband while we were on the train to let him know that they would have a guest for the evening. The smooth metal door had no knobs or hinges, only a number, 210. She had only to place a finger on the touch pad next to it and the door slid open instantly receding into the wall. Rachel rushed in first, followed by her mother and then me.

The apartment was comfortably but modestly furnished. There were no windows in most of these residential units, but they did have a couple of manually operated escape hatches for emergency egress. The material and construction of these buildings made it almost impossible for them to ever burn or collapse in an earthquake. Large high resolution video screens covered nearly an entire wall in most rooms. The video screen displayed beautiful natural scenes such as a mountain lake, the Grand Canyon, and a Hawaiian beach. The image was so vivid and real looking that I felt I could walk right into it. I learned that they were simply giant computer monitors in which all entertainment, information, communication and data processing could be displayed.

Rachel turned into a hallway and went in what I supposed was her bedroom.

"Dinner in a half hour!" Helen shouted to her just before her door swished shut.

Then a moment later, I heard the sound of another door opening from down the same hallway. A man emerged into the main room.

He appeared to be at least my age or maybe a few years older. He had thinning and receding hair, a medium build and wore the clothes of an office worker or mid-level manager. Helen looked at him lovingly and he looked at me with curiosity.

"Darling, this is Joshua McNeal. Joshua, this is my husband, Carl."

I offered him my extended hand. He grasped it in a short but friendly shake.

"He was having trouble with the I.D. System, and I thought maybe you could advise him."

"Trouble? What kind of trouble?" Carl questioned.

"The fact is that I'm not in the system. I was born here, but I've been away for many years." I explained.

"You're not registered anywhere?" Carl probed.

But before I could answer, Helen stepped in.

"Why don't we discuss it over dinner?"

It was agreed, so Carl and I sat down at the oval table next to the kitchen. Helen grabbed four flat rectangular trays from the refrigerator and placed them into a Warmer/Processor. They looked similar to the same type of frozen dinners that I was used to eating. But when they came out of the processor, the food tripled in volume, piled up looking fresh and steaming hot. They were turkey dinners with thick cut meat, stuffing, mashed potatoes and gravy, garden peas, cranberry sauce and topped with a fresh warm, buttered roll. She pressed a button next to an intercom and called her daughter to dinner.

Helen and Rachel served the meal which included a cold glass of herbal tea. The meal in front of me looked and smelled delicious. I was curious about the processor because this food was not just warmed like in a microwave, but it was fresh like homemade. The ladies took their seats at the table. Helen nodded to Carl and then he and his family bowed their heads. I knew what was happening, so I bowed my head also.

"Lord, thank you for this meal and for all of your blessings. Please bless it and all of us who partake of it, in Jesus name, amen."

Everyone said amen, including me because I was in complete agreement with Carl's prayer. I was indeed grateful for the food, and to be in the company of such kind and hospitable people. Then they started digging into their food, so I did likewise, although Rachel was doing more poking than eating. After a few minutes, Carl came up with a question for me.

"Joshua, do you have family anywhere?"

"No, not anymore." I answered in a tone that hopefully would not cause him to pity me.

"No family anywhere, mother, father, sister, brother?"

"Carl." Helen interjected, thinking that her husband was being a bit too pushy.

"No, it's alright. You need to know everything about me to have any chance of helping me."

"Did you ever register with I.D. Services?" Carl asked.

"No, I never did." I answered flatly.

"Protest?" He questioned.

"You could say that."

"Darling, why don't we work on this after dinner?" Helen asked Carl.

I got the feeling that Carl and Helen were concerned that the discussion would lead into sensitive areas that they would rather their young daughter did not hear about.

"Joshua, why don't you tell us about yourself? Whatever you are comfortable sharing." Helen asked gently. And I could tell that she was truly interested.

I felt at ease with these people, and I determined that they had a right to know more about the stranger that they had invited into their home. So I opened up to them in all sincerity.

"Well, my father owned and operated a small hardware store in Glendale. I remember that he was not home very often. We actually didn't get along very well most of the time. I mean, he didn't smack me around or anything like that."

Rachel chuckled.

"Rachel." Helen chided her daughter.

"Sorry." Rachel said while still snickering.

I think my face turned red as I just remembered the current double meaning of the word smack.

"I mean he was critical of me most of the time. I couldn't do much right as far as he was concerned. When I was in high school, I worked at the store one summer. Well, that was the last time. My mother, on the other hand, was very supportive of me and encouraged me in whatever I tried to do. She was the typical Jewish mother who would brag about her boy."

"Oh, you're Jewish?" Helen interrupted.

"My mother was. But when I was about Rachel's age, all of us flew to a family reunion in Ohio. Ever since then, I knew exactly what I wanted to do with my life. I wanted to fly."

"Fly?" Carl questioned.

"Yes, I wanted to fly the latest and fastest aircraft made. I built model airplanes and read everything about them. All I could think about is that I wanted to be a pilot or an astronaut. In college, I joined the R.O.T.C. and struggled to keep my grades up so I could get into the Air Force Academy."

"Air Force Academy?" Carl questioned again with an increasingly puzzled look on his face.

"Yes, the United States Air Force Academy in Colorado Springs, Colorado. When I got the letter of acceptance, it was the second happiest day of my life."

"What was the happiest day?" Helen asked.

"That was the very next day when my girl, Kathy agreed to be my wife."

"Oh, that's sweet." Helen remarked with a big smile.

"So after graduating from the Academy, I trained to be a fighter pilot, some years later, I became a test pilot."

I could clearly see that I was losing Carl. The look of incredulity on his face was so strong that his very eyes were like a knife stabbing me. So I paused, looked them both in the eye, and began to speak in the most sincere tone that I could.

"Everything I told you was the truth. But I didn't tell you

everything. I trust you both, and I am going to trust you with a secret about me that could cost me my freedom or even my life."

"Wait." Helen interrupted again.

"Rachel, do you have homework?"

"No, we have testing this week."

"Then go to your room and study until bedtime."

Rachel got up and went straight to her room without a word. I think that she was bored by the whole adult conversation anyway. Helen listened for Rachel's door to close. Then she turned back to me.

"Go ahead, Joshua."

"Helen, when you were helping me input information at the terminal this afternoon, there was one bit of vital information that I did not give you, that was the year I was born."

"Yes, why were you having such trouble with that?" She asked.

"Because, I was born in the year 1995."

They both stared at me and each other for a few long seconds.

"I have to say you sure look well preserved for 101 year old man." Carl quipped, but without a smile.

"How is that possible?" Helen asked skeptically.

"I know it sounds incredible, but you need to hear the whole story."

"You have our complete attention." Carl said as he folded his hands on the table in front of him.

I took a deep breath and then began to tell my story.

"It was late fall, the holiday season of the year 2031. I was working at Edwards Air Force Base and we were living in Lancaster at the time. My wife and daughter were driving home late. They had spent the day with her parents. It was her mother's birthday. I had to work that day. Anyway, they were riding in the I.C.C."

"What's the I.C.C.?" Helen asked.

"Intelligent Car Corridor, it was a special lane along the highway that had barriers on both sides and was only for the new hybrid vehicles with auto drive. The cruising speed in the corridor was 80 to 90 miles per hour. The car was only about a year old. It was an electric, hydrogen hybrid. My wife drove it most of the time. For me, I was perfectly happy with my old eight cylinder gas burning pick-up truck."

"You had two vehicles?" Carl asked in amazement.

"Yeah, but that was pretty typical in those days."

I felt the pain coming back and my chest tighten as I was about to recount what happened next.

"The car ahead of them came up to a curve in the road, but something went wrong. Instead of turning into the curve, the car rolled up the barrier and became airborne. It fell right in front of my wife's car. There was no time to adjust. It was all over in a split second. The hydrogen tanks in both vehicles ignited in a fiery explosion. There was nothing left."

I paused for a moment to try and regain my composure. But I had to go on, not for the purpose of gaining their sympathy, but to explain to them what motivated me to accept this unusual and dangerous mission.

"Suddenly, I found myself alone and devastated. I must have asked God a thousand times. Why my girls? Why not some criminal or corrupt politician? Why my girls?"

I had to stop. Both of their faces expressed sadness for me. Helen was almost to the point of tears.

"I'm sorry; I didn't mean to dwell on that. After all, it happened 65 years ago."

"Joshua." Helen said softly, putting her hand on mine.

"A nuclear pulse engine was developed for spacecraft. It could propel a vehicle through space many times faster than conventional rocket engines. But it was dangerous and not completely predictable. The Air Force and some Government contractors thought that the new engine would be powerful enough to test Einstein's theory of time travel."

"Time travel?" Carl questioned.

"Well, relativity. The theory states that speed can affect time. There were too many variables to launch an unmanned craft, it could be lost and nobody would ever know what happened. So they needed a human pilot, a volunteer. When they asked me, I was more than happy to leave a world that no longer held anything for me."

"Are you telling us that they had the technology 60 some years ago to propel a man through time?" Carl asked while squinting at me skeptically.

"Well, they hoped they did. You see, an experiment like that can never really be proven by the people who conducted it, because even if it worked, they would probably never know it."

"That's just too hard to believe." Carl insisted.

"There are more things in Heaven and Earth than are dreamt of in your philosophy, Horatio." I quoted with a touch of drama.

"Who's Horatio?" Carl was thrown a little off balance by my quote from Hamlet.

"Shakespeare, isn't it?" Helen interjected like a precocious school girl.

"Very good." I said with a smile.

But I did not want to lose either of them. So in all seriousness, I looked Carl directly in the eyes.

"I realize that it sounds unbelievable, almost as unbelievable as the world I came back to. Everything has changed. My world, the world that I knew is gone. You are the first people I met since my return that I felt free to tell my story. If I were trying to deceive you, would I make up such an unbelievable story?"

Carl sat back in his chair and stared into space, lost in deep thought. After a moment, he looked straight at me.

"You know, I have a direct link to my company's computer from my home computer. My company can access Government data bases that are not available to the general public. These include archived video and sites from the old Internet. I wonder if I searched the historical archives that I might find you there."

I was fascinated, but a little nervous. Since most of my work for the Air Force was top secret, it would not have been publicized. Still, there must be something about me on the Internet. I did have a Facebook page which I seldom maintained, and I closed it when I joined the Air Force. The accident with my wife and daughter was reported on several LA stations. We all moved into the small living room and sat down in front of the huge monitor.

Carl picked up his small control unit which included a keypad and voice controlled command functions. He used the keypad to enter passwords and filter through about four steps to get to the archive menu that he sought. He looked toward me.

"What was your rank?"

"Major."

"What is your full name?"

"Joshua Samuel McNeal." I said distinctly as Carl typed it in.

Carl typed in Major Joshua Samuel McNeal United States Air Force. The letters appeared large on the screen. Then he hit SEARCH. Instantly, three possibilities appeared. All of whom were Majors in the U.S. Air Force with my exact name, but covering a period of almost one hundred years. As we read the blurbs under those names, one of them referred to the death of astronaut Major Joshua McNeal in 2034.

He selected it and immediately the screen went to an old network news story dated September 7, 2034. A female reporter sat in studio and told the story.

"This just in… A spokesman from NASA has just disclosed that a mysterious and tragic explosion has occurred on a Martian supply shuttle. The experimental interplanetary vessel was on a mission to re-supply the Martian space station, *ICARUS*. The lone pilot, Major Joshua McNeal is presumed lost along with the spacecraft. The cause for the explosion is not yet known. Major McNeal was a 17 year veteran of the U.S. Air Force. His wife and young daughter were killed three years earlier in an automobile accident on a Los Angeles area freeway."

When she mentioned my name, a picture of me came up on the screen. It was my service portrait with me in my dress blue uniform.

"Oh my…" Helen gasped as she saw my picture flash up on the screen.

Carl sat there with his eyes and mouth wide open. In truth, we were all stunned by what we saw and heard. But it all made sense.

When Flight Control could no longer track me, the Government had to disguise the top secret experiment as a routine supply mission. A tragic accident would account for the loss of a spacecraft and a pilot.

"It's true." Helen admitted, but still shocked by the revelation.

Carl had seen enough to convince him. He switched off the computer and sat there in silence for a couple of minutes, deep in thought.

"You were right to avoid the authorities. They would have accused you of being an insurgent, a criminal for not registering." Carl paused again, still thinking about my situation.

"And even if they had researched your story and found it to be true, I think they would have made you disappear. It has happened many times before. Sometimes people just disappear and are never heard from again." Carl admitted with somber resignation.

"It's really that bad?" I probed.

"It is, and it's getting worse."

Then Carl suddenly had a puzzled look on his face.

"By the way, how did you manage to get into the city? Where did you land?

"I made an emergency landing in the Santa Barbara Channel a couple miles off shore. The ship sank but it was equipped with a small rubber raft which brought me to shore."

"What did you do when you got on shore?"

"I followed the coast in an eastward direction."

"But that's all quarantined area. Everything is destroyed. There's no food or water, it's fenced off and patrolled by police."

"Tell me about it."

"What do you mean?"

"I mean it took me four days to get through that Hellhole, stretching my rations as far as they would go, and then fighting the rats for the rest. I slept in caves and abandoned buildings, dodging police hoppers and drones all the way."

"But how did you get over the fence?"

"I didn't go over it. I went under it, through an old abandoned storm drain pipe which terminated just outside the city."

"Incredible." Carl said while shaking his head.

"It was a miracle." Helen added.

"Yes and the Air Force Survival Training Course didn't hurt."

"Unfortunately, your struggle is not over. I can't put you in the system. The only way that you can be registered is to walk into an I.D.S. office and be interviewed by one of their agents. And in your case, I wouldn't recommend it." Carl declared plainly.

"What alternative do I have?" I asked.

"Very few, I'm afraid. You see, in spite of our clean, modern cities and all of the talk of world unity and the so-called New Era; we are living in the most complete police state the world has ever known. And you never know who you can trust. It's gotten to the point where half the people are policing the other half."

"Well then, I guess I better just keep on moving." I said with sad resignation.

Then Carl leaned in close to me and began to speak in a soft and guarded tone.

"There is a kind of underground, mostly Christians who keep track of what the police are doing and give warning when necessary. I know of a man who runs a small assembly shop east of the city. The larger Government contractors occasionally piece out work to him, so the police don't hassle him. He has been known to help people move out to the Freelands."

"What are the Freelands?"

"They're towns and settlements up in the hills and in the countryside where people live completely outside of the world economic system. I mean, they are on their own, they fend for themselves."

"How does the Government allow that?"

"For one thing, most of them are heavily armed. Many are the remnants of the Christian militias. There was an agreement some years ago, a kind of treaty that the Government made with them that if they would end the hostilities, they could live apart from the rest of society."

"I don't think that's going to last very long."

"Neither do I. Especially with Sheyer now head of the World Council."

"Who's Sheyer?"

"Renard Sheyer, a French Iranian who forsook his Muslim roots in favor of an amalgamated religion which he claims is the ultimate evolution of all the world religions."

"Really?"

"Yes, but what he has no tolerance for are people who hold firmly to their faith, namely Christians and Jews. His rhetoric is becoming more and more vile and dangerous. And he's growing in popularity. Tens of thousands rally every time he makes a speech, and he's on ILink and WorldNet almost every day."

"It sounds like this guy is going to eventually make things rough for you and your family. Why don't you try to get your family out to the Freelands?"

"Because that is a rough, hard existence which none of us are equipped for. I'm not a fighter or a hunter or a farmer. I've never even fired a gun. I'm a computer programmer. That's all I know." Carl argued while ending his statement by lowering his eyes in shame.

"I'm sorry Carl. I had no right to suggest that."

"You can sleep on the sofa tonight. After breakfast, I'll give you directions to the shop I told you about. The train will take you most of the way, but I'm afraid you'll have to walk the rest of the way. Well, I'm going to turn in now. Good night." With that, Carl got up and disappeared down the hall.

Helen reached out to me and put her hand on my arm.

"Joshua, I know that your wife and daughter are with Jesus and they are alive with Him. I also know that God has his hand on you and has miraculously protected you for some purpose. Don't you think?"

I placed my hand on her hand.

"I think that Carl is the luckiest man I know."

I smiled at her, got up and moved toward the sofa. She got up and moved toward the hallway.

"Good night, Joshua."

"Good night, Helen."

Morning came early and I woke up as soon as Helen came in and turned on the kitchen lights. Breakfast was prepared much faster than I was used to. Carl and Rachel eventually wandered in and sat down at the table. I followed directly after to see a beautiful plate of scrambled eggs, sausage and toast, together with hot coffee and orange juice.

After breakfast, everyone was in a rush to go different directions. Helen was taking Rachel out to catch the school shuttle. Carl was about to retreat to his office computer, but not before he handed me a print out which contained public information about the assembly shop he was sending me to. Carl made sure that there was no way to identify whose computer printed the page, and we solemnly agreed that I would never disclose where I got it.

I thanked the Jensen's the best I could, but nothing would be adequate. As I left their apartment building and walked toward the train station, I thought that I would never see them again, but I certainly would never forget them.

CHAPTER 6

FUGITIVE

I sat in the train on a seat by myself. Anxious thoughts filled my mind. I hardly looked out the window and I did not speak to anyone. When the train stopped at my destination, I almost failed to disembark in time. But this was partially due to the fact that so many of the towns and streets that I used to know had their names changed or were absorbed into the Metroplex. My best reckoning placed me somewhere in what used to be the San Gabriel Valley.

After swallowing a couple cups of cold water in the station, I made my way down to the street level and started walking in an eastward direction. The moving sidewalks had ended at that point so I had to proceed the old fashioned way. There were a few small retail outlets along the street and a few of what I used to know as convenience stores. These were dispersed among small and medium size service shops of various kinds. As I continued down the main street, I did not recognize any residential structures. The buildings themselves seemed to age in style and construction the further out

I went. I noticed the familiar concrete tilt-up buildings and even a few of the old stucco on wood frame types.

There were far fewer people on the sidewalk out here than in the city, but there were more large service and delivery vehicles on the street. Occasionally, I saw a police hopper roll by. They did not fly unless they were answering a specific call. When I saw them, I would just keep walking, look straight ahead, and try not to act too concerned. Eventually, I found myself in an all industrial area. Most of the buildings were older in this part of town, not so much the clean, streamline and uniform designs of the city.

It was fall, my favorite season and a cool, dry breeze was blowing. I was actually enjoying my walk because these surroundings made me feel more like I was back home than at any other time since my return. But on every block or so were erected large, high definition video billboards which continually displayed public service announcements and what I considered Government propaganda. These billboards were of the type that I knew in my time, except every so often they would project a holographic image that seemed to jump off the screen and come to life in virtual 3D. One such image was that of the man himself, Renard Sheyer speaking to the World Council in Brussels. The caption under it read; The North American League supports a united world. That cold slap in the face just reminded me that I was not back home.

Carl's print out had a map of the area around the shop called Keller Fabrication. That was my destination. At that point, most of the larger cross streets were numbered. I was coming up to 17th street and the shop was on 22nd street. There was still another hour of daylight left as I turned south on 22nd street.

In a few blocks, I was getting a completely different perspective. There were abandoned, boarded up shops and factories to my right and to my left. The vehicle traffic was very light and the road itself looked like it had not been repaired for decades. I was even surprised to see fenced off empty lots overgrown with weeds. That was a sight one would never see in the city. This, I imagined was just one of the many graveyards of the businesses which did not survive the financial upheavals or the Government take overs. These ghost towns have been left here in the outlying areas, out of sight and out of mind, but a reminder to anyone who sees them that the past was truly dead.

The building was small for a factory, perhaps 18,000 sq. ft. The construction was concrete outer walls with only one loading dock that I could see and one simple glass door for the front office. It was painted grey many years ago with only a simple painted sign near the top of the wall facing the street to identify it. The shape was rectangular, simple, plain but functional. Aesthetically speaking, it would have been quite unimpressive even in my time. The building was situated between an empty lot on the left containing only the foundation slab of a former building, and a very large but abandoned warehouse with many loading docks on the right. The roll-up door was open and I could see some people working inside. There were a few vehicles in the worn out and weathered parking lot. I walked into the front office.

"Hi, can I help you?" I was greeted by a thirty something man with a beard, tattoos on his arms and a small gold ring in one ear. He appeared to be looking for something in the front office and in a hurry to get somewhere else.

"I'm looking for the owner."

"That would be Mr. Keller, but he's not here. I can tell you, if you're looking for a job, we're not hiring right now."

"I need to discuss a personal matter with Mr. Keller."

"Personal Matter? Who are you? What's your name?"

"My name is Joshua McNeal."

"Hold on, I'll see if he's out in back." He pulled out his phone, scrolled and tapped the screen.

"John, there's a Joshua McNeal up front to see you."

"I don't know a Joshua McNeal. Who is he with?" John Keller's voice came in loud and clear over the phone speaker.

"He says it's a personal matter."

"Alright, I'll be up in a minute."

"He'll be right up, just wait here." The young man turned around and went back into the shop area.

After a couple of minutes, a man walked into the front office. He looked to be almost 60 years old. He had a full head of hair and a neatly trimmed beard which were mostly grey. His clothes were casual, which did not hide a moderately extended stomach. He looked at me intensely but maintained a neutral expression.

"I'm John Keller. What can I do for you?" He said flatly, not extending a welcoming hand. He just stood there in front of me ready to scrutinize my every word and movement. I knew I had to be very forthcoming with this man because his gaze seemed to pierce through to my soul.

"My name is Joshua McNeal. Some very kind Christian people sent me here, although I will not say who they are. They said maybe you could help me."

"Are you a Christian?"

"Truthfully, I cannot say that I am."

"I see. What kind of help do you need?"

"I want to get out of the city. I want to get to the Freelands."

"What makes you think that I can help with that?"

"I just thought… I guess… Maybe I made a mistake. I'm sorry to trouble you, sir." My heart sunk within me as I prepared myself to be on my own again.

I turned to leave.

"Wait; let me scan your I.D. card." He said as he turned on the small terminal on the counter which was there to receive payments from will call customers.

I walked slowly back toward him.

"I don't have an I.D. card."

"You mean you don't have it on you?"

"I mean I don't have one, never had one. I have never been registered."

He looked at me for a few seconds. I could not tell what he was thinking or what he was going to do. Then he asked me to come back into his office. He sat behind his desk and I pulled up a chair in front of the desk. Keller opened a drawer and pulled out a round, black electronic device. It was a Government issue D.N.A. hand scanner. He slid it in front of me.

"You know what this is?"

"Yes, I think so."

"Ok, put your fingers together, make your hand flat and put it in." I did so as he looked at his computer monitor.

"Take it out, wait a couple seconds, and then try it again."

I repeated the action until the disbelieving scowl faded from his face.

"You're right. You're not in the system."

"No sir."

"You know, there are only three categories of people that have never registered: Christian separatists, wanted criminals, and anti-Government insurgents."

Since I did not feel it appropriate to introduce a fourth option of time traveler, I held my peace.

"Are you a hater, a xenophobe, a Neanderthal, an anti-Government agitator, a threat to world peace and unity?"

"Every chance I get." He smiled slightly at my remark.

"Well then, I guess you've come to the right place. But since you're not registered, I can't hire you or even officially acknowledge your existence. There's an order we're working on right now. It will be finished in about a week. They are aircraft parts going to Las Vegas for the Government Fleet Service Center."

"Nellis or McCarran?" My question elicited a strange look on his face.

"You must have been in elementary school when Nellis Air Force Base was closed down. And the old McCarran Airport was converted to the Dumas Fleet Service Center about ten years ago. It's kind of strange that you would refer to them by their old names."

"Well, I'm kind of a history buff."

"I guess so. But anyway, you'll stay here the whole time until the order is ready to ship. We'll provide food and a place to sleep.

We can also come up with a few little chores for you to do while you're here."

"Be happy to."

"When the van is loaded, you'll go in the back with it."

"To Vegas?"

"No, about half way up the Cajon Pass, the driver will pull off and stop for breakfast. He'll park off in a remote corner of the lot. He will knock three times on the side of the van before he goes into the café. You wait about ten minutes then sneak out the back door and close it behind you. You'll have to make your way to the old highway. It's closed to vehicles but you can walk it. After about 12 or 15 miles of an uphill walk, you should arrive at the Wrightwood Camp. Now, I can't promise they'll take you in, but your chances are good. It's not an easy life, but you're still young and strong. You should be alright."

"I don't know how to thank you."

"The only way is just to remember that when you do get out, you never heard of this place or me and I never heard of you. Agreed?"

"Agreed."

We shook hands and then he showed me the loft above the shop floor where I would spend the next several nights. It was small, dusty and filled with boxes of archived business records. There was a clearing in the middle about 8 feet by 8 feet. He commandeered a couple of old furniture pads from the delivery vans to serve as my bed. It was not the most luxurious of accommodations, but it was out of the way and out of sight. I was grateful.

The shop employed about 20 workers, mostly men but some women also. He kept his lunchroom stocked with easy to prepare food and drink. I would usually go in between the scheduled breaks and help myself. Because of the size of the company, it was impossible to avoid contact with the other workers. But I tried to keep my interactions short and superficial so to avoid bringing up questions that I would rather not answer.

Most of the tasks I performed were low skill manual labor. I would help with loading and unloading deliveries, stock supplies, run the power sweeper and even clean the restrooms at night. Keller ordered a new set of rugged work clothes for me with no markings on them of course. Nobody wore uniforms or labelled clothing at his factory. He was also generous enough to let me use the shower in his private bathroom attached to his office.

Every so often I would wander over to the main assembly area to see how the Las Vegas order was coming along. The product was a hydraulic pump used to power the operation of flaps on jet aircraft. I spoke to the female foreman in the assembly area. She seemed impressed that I was able to identify the part right away and to ask some knowledgeable questions about it. I did find out that completion was only two days away.

The next morning, sometime after the first break, I went into the lunchroom for a toasted bagel and coffee. Someone had left the large monitor on. The screen was embedded in the wall near the ceiling. It was tuned to World Net News, so as I was preparing my breakfast, I listened. Again, the story centered on Sheyer. It was something about a treaty with Israel. I was alone in the lunchroom, but a moment after I sat down, Keller walked in, said hello to me and moved toward the coffee machine. He also took notice of the news report on the monitor.

It seemed that for years, Israel stood alone among all other nations in resisting inclusion into any multi-national federation. They have also resisted the intrusion of the World Council and the World Court upon their sovereignty. But this treaty, brokered by Sheyer himself, would bring Israel into the family of nations ultimately under the authority of the World Council. In return, Israel would be protected from military invasion and maintain a degree of national sovereignty, at least for seven years.

"So he's the one." Keller muttered as he watched the story to the end.

He held his coffee cup in one hand and switched off the monitor with the other. Then he took a seat at the table across from me.

"The one what?"

"The one that was prophesied. The one that will soon take peace from the Earth and plunge it into darkness."

"You mean, the Anti-Christ?"

"Do you know about that?"

"Yes, I've heard."

"This is his first major action. He will do things that nobody else could do before and the whole world will embrace him. Well, not quite the whole world."

"But he just made a peace treaty with Israel."

"He'll break it. But before that, he's going to try and eliminate the real fly in his soup."

"What's that?"

"The Christians. He hates us. The world hates us. We are their last impediment from ushering in a godless, humanistic utopia on Earth."

"Isn't there anything we can do?"

"From my perspective as a Christian, just try to survive until the Lord returns."

"What about fighting back?"

"Some will choose that. I guess we will all resist him in our own way."

His demeanor turned to melancholy as he rose and walked slowly to the door. He stopped and turned back to me.

"We're finishing the Vegas order. We'll be loading it up the day after tomorrow, early in the morning. Be ready."

"I will... Mr. Keller."

"John."

"John, I really don't know how to thank you. You're taking a big risk doing this for me. I'm in your debt."

He didn't say anything else. He just looked at me as if to say good luck, and then he left the room.

The next day the shop was busy. Custom wooden crates were being made for the Las Vegas order and I was actually allowed to help cut and assemble the crates. It felt good to be engaged in constructive work. I was both excited and nervous about leaving tomorrow. The plan was that only Keller and the driver would know that I was to stow away with the cargo. There was a large oil storage tank against the fence opposite the loading dock. Before sunrise, I was to hide behind that tank until the van was loaded. When the loading was finished, I had to quickly sneak inside. The driver would then close the door behind me. Any worker who inquired about my absence would be told that I left to take another job. And since I have only been there a few days, it would not raise much suspicion

It was early afternoon, shortly after lunch break and the whole shop was noisy and busy. But suddenly the noise subsided and the people stopped working to look at some very important strangers who had entered the shop. In the forefront was an Asian man wearing a casual uniform like a city official. He had a shield badge pinned to his shirt and his official identification hanging around his neck. He held a small case in one hand. He was not armed, but there were two police officers behind him in full body armor, helmet and face shield, who were. One of the officers stood near the door to the front office and the other strategically placed himself by the loading door. His hopper could be seen parked in the loading area. I turned to the worker next to me and quietly asked her what was going on. She told me that it was a random inspection. I thought at first that it was an inspection of the products before they shipped out, or maybe an inspection of the shop itself. It turned out to be neither. The Government inspector was there to check the people.

I broke out into a cold sweat when I saw him start to systematically go from person to person in the shop and scan their I.D. cards. There was nothing for me to do. I couldn't run out and I couldn't sneak out. This was it, I thought to myself. Still, I had to play it cool. I couldn't tip my hand prematurely. If an opportunity did present itself, I had to wait for it. I prayed silently and desperately on the inside while projecting an indifferent attitude on the outside. He was only two workers away from me, then one, and then he stood in front of me. The reader was no larger than a cell phone. He held it out to me.

"Scan your I.D. card, please." He said in perfect English. .

"I lost it."

"You lost it?"

"Yeah, I was out in back loading an order and I had to break down a pallet. I reached in my pocket for a knife to cut the strap and my I.D. card came out with it. Unfortunately, it fell down the sewer grate and was lost. I just didn't have time to get a new one."

"Did you inform your employer about this?"

"No, I was just going to take care of it on my next day off."

"You know they just increased the fine for not having your I.D. card to 250 credits."

"I didn't know that. But I planned to replace it as soon as possible."

He didn't say anything for a moment and I thought that maybe he had accepted my story and would move on. But instead he found a nearby table and set down the case that he held in his hand. He opened the case and removed a portable DNA scanner. The monitor screen was on the inside lid of the case. He told me to come over and insert my hand. I knew the routine. As expected, he came up with no results. Then he asked me a series of questions; my name, where I was born, where I was registered and of course my birthdate. I only lied about where I was registered and the year of my birth. Since I was 40 years old, I told him that I was born in 2056.

After he input the information I gave him, he scanned my hand again, and again as expected showed no results.

"We have a problem here. We're going to have to bring you in for questioning."

I tried to act calm and not appear to be a threat which would put him and the cops on their guard. He told me to go over and stand by the officer closest to me which was by the loading dock. As I walked calmly toward the officer, every eye in the place was on me. My military training taught me to assess the situation quickly and to engage a plan of attack with the highest probability of success. The officer stood with his back to the loading dock. The ramp was retracted so it was about a four foot drop from the dock to the concrete pavement outside.

The officer told me to put my hands on the wall and spread my legs. His voice came through loud and clear from micro speakers in his helmet and visor. I complied, hoping that his helmet would obscure his peripheral vision just enough. He began to search my upper body. When he stooped down to pat my legs, I made my move. With speed enhanced by adrenalin, I turned and pulled his gun out of the holster and with my free arm I pushed him back off the loading dock. He landed on his back which knocked the wind out of him. He lay there squirming, gasping for breath, but he did not get up. Next, I moved quickly to the other officer, pointing the gun at him. He raised his hands. Thankfully, he did not go for his weapon because these firearms were strange to me. The barrel housing was rectangular but twice as high as a normal semi-automatic pistol. It had two barrels, one over the other.

I ordered him to take off his helmet because I knew that he could immediately communicate with his station, if he hadn't already. He did so and then I told him to face the wall and put his hands up on it. After he did, I removed his weapon and shoved it in my pocket. I aimed the other pistol at the helmet on the floor and fired in an attempt to disable it. Some of the workers moved back. What came out of the barrel was an electric stun dart. It made almost no sound when fired except when it hit and bounced off the visor, throwing a few sparks. There was a slider switch on the side of the weapon which was in the backward position. I slid it to the forward position and immediately a laser sight came on projecting a bright red dot on whatever I pointed at. I took another shot at the helmet and the familiar pop of a live 9mm round burst out causing some to scream and the visor to shatter.

I knew that I couldn't hold them off for long. Keeping my eye and the weapon on the officer, I slowly crept back toward the loading dock. The other officer was still lying on his back, breathing but not moving much. He was just a few yards away from his parked hopper. I jumped off the dock and ran to the hopper. The indicators were still lit and active. The officer had left his I.D. card in the slot on the panel. The wheel was a hybrid of an airplane stick and motorcycle handle bars. Thankfully, the controls were simple and straight forward. I threw the weapon I was holding in the rear seat, which I assumed was for prisoners since it faced backwards and had arm and leg restraints which opened and closed mechanically.

Wasting no more time, I got into the driver seat and looked at the large display just above the wheel. There it was, in the control menu; FLY AUTO and FLY MANUAL. I chose FLY AUTO for the time being until I got a good feel for the vehicle. I heard the jets fire up. There were four computer controlled jets on swivel arms which controlled speed, rate of climb, pitch and roll. I turned up the throttle while pulling slightly back on the wheel and I was airborne. In a few seconds I had cleared the parking lot, crossed the street and was flying over the roofs of buildings. The vehicle was smooth and responsive. The computer adjusted instantly to my control of the wheel. It was such a pleasure to fly that I almost forgot that I was running for my life.

After I felt confident enough to stop watching the display screen, I noticed that I was heading east. But where should I go? The police would be right on my heels. If I remained over open, level ground, it would be easy for them to overtake me. Then I looked to the hills and mountains to the north. That was it! I could hide among the peaks and canyons and the authorities might not chase me too far into what they considered to be hostile territory. Wrightwood Camp was too far, but I thought maybe I could find a friendly colony in the local hills. I banked left and headed north at full speed.

The hopper would bounce a radar signal down and forward instantly mapping out the topography and any obstacles on the ground. The on-board computer would immediately adjust throttle and pitch to fly over them at a relatively constant altitude. That characteristic of following the contours of the ground makes the vehicle seem to bounce up and down in flight, thus the nickname hopper. It felt and operated just like a motorcycle whether in flight or on the ground. They could not be considered a true aircraft and they had their limitations for altitude and distance in flight. But they were simple to master and could go just about anywhere, truly remarkable vehicles.

The ground was sloping up rapidly as I approached the foothills. When I looked back toward the city, I saw two hoppers speeding across the horizon from the south. They were in fast pursuit only about two miles back. I rounded the first hill and flew in the canyons as long as I could, only flying over the hills when I had to. When I did fly over a summit, I gave away my position. The two hoppers were closing the distance behind me. The climbing and the speed were spending fuel at a rapid rate. They were closing in. Fortunately, these vehicles were not equipped with built in guns like a fighter plane, so there would be little they could do if they caught up to me. I kept wondering though, how long would it be before a real military aircraft joined the pursuit.

I figured that I must be somewhere in the hills above what used to be Pasadena or Glendale. I had come full circle, it seemed. The irony did not escape me. I saw them again. They were flying low as possible, maintaining a steady constant speed. I decided to switch to FLY MANUAL where I would make all the adjustments myself and the computer would only execute them. A decision had to be made quickly. The two pursuing hoppers were rounding the last hill and meandering up the canyon right on my tail. I decided to push the vehicle to its power limits by climbing up into the higher elevations. My climb pitch was about 45 degrees and I had passed the 5000 foot elevation. Pine forests were under me and all around me. While still climbing, I was looking around for a flat clearing to ditch the hopper because my fuel was getting dangerously low.

It seemed like the two police hoppers were deliberately slowing their chase. I saw them following me around the mountain, but at about 1000 feet below me. Their strategy made sense. They were waiting for me to run out of fuel. My display screen was flashing red, telling me that I had five minutes of fuel left. Desperately I searched for a place, any place to land the thing. The trees were too close together on the flat areas and the slopes were too steep where there were fewer trees. Then I heard a loud audio alarm like a constant bong sound. It was alerting me that I had only 60 seconds of fuel left. There was no time and no choice left. I found the least steep part of the slope, one with vegetation growing on it. I pulled in as close as possible. I climbed up on the seat and just as the engines shut down, I jumped off into a bush.

As I held on, I turned and watched the hopper slide rapidly down the slope. The hopper flew off the slope and over a sheer cliff. But climbing up that cliff were my two pursuers who had momentarily lost sight of me. My hopper landed squarely on one of the officer's vehicle. There was a crash and a huge fireball. The officer died instantly. The other one was shaken but was in control enough to descend the mountain and head back toward the city.

The sight stunned me. But I had crossed the Rubicon and could never go back. Not only was I a fugitive for being a dissident, but I would from that moment on, be blamed for the death of a police officer. I had to hide in the forest like an animal. There was no doubt in my mind that they would pursue me with aircraft, drones and anything else they could get their hands on. The slope was climbable as long as you didn't slip. I grabbed hold of bushes and weeds until I made my way into the dense forest where it was not so steep. My immediate goal was to get as deep into the forest as I could before dark. It did reassure me to feel the police pistol in my pocket, but that would not protect me from the cold or hunger or thirst. When it became too dark for me to continue safely, I found a large tree and huddled down on the uphill side of it. Eventually, I fell asleep.

CHAPTER 7

ANGEL CAMP

Kathy and Audrey were talking and laughing about something as they drove home in the car. They were not really looking where they were going. They didn't have to. The car was in the Intelligent Car Corridor on Auto Drive. I can see their smiles and hear their laughter.

"What shall we get Daddy for Christmas? Audrey asked.

Perhaps Kathy glanced briefly out the front windshield to see the vehicle fly right into them. No time to think. No time to pray. Snuffed out in an instant fiery explosion.

I woke up with my face in a bed of dried pine needles. I don't know what really happened that night, but I've had several versions of that same dream come back to haunt me again and again. Each time it awakens me, I look around to see if it was only a nightmare, if my wife and daughter are waiting for me in the next room.   But then I realize that it was all too real, and I die a little all over again.

I lay on the cold ground and cried. I cried until I had no more left to cry out and then I just spent more time thinking and remembering.

After about a half hour I rose to my feet. The sun was up but the morning air was still very chilly. The trees were so thick and full that I could not even tell directions from the sun. But direction didn't really matter at that point. I followed the slope of the mountain upward while trying to find the smoothest trail up. My immediate need was for water. There were many seasonal streams in these mountains. With the larger streams, you could hear the water running, but the smaller streams you could not. The key was to look for natural depressions or gullies where water could flow.

It was about mid-morning and I was climbing and listening as I went. I heard a steady noise, but it wasn't running water. It was more mechanical, like an aircraft. I looked up trying to see the open sky through the trees but it was difficult. The sound was much quieter than any helicopter I had known, but it persisted. I stopped and looked up again between the trees. Then I saw it. It was a small rotary wing craft. It was a military drone, zig zagging its way up and down the mountain. I had no doubt what it was searching for. Those drones, unlike the stealth drones that I encountered before, were armed with small laser guided missiles that could take out a target remotely. All I could do is hug a tree trunk and stay perfectly still until I didn't hear it anymore.

I waited and waited as the drone flew back and forth over my position. I thought about trying to shoot it down, but there were only split seconds when I had a clear shot and if I missed, I would only give away my position. I remained still.

After about 15 minutes, I did not see it or hear it anymore. As I climbed, I realized that I was getting thirsty, but not to the point that it would stop me. The location was beautiful and peaceful. But I was not in a state of mind to appreciate it. Endurance did pay off, sometime in the afternoon; I found a small stream flowing almost vertically down a rocky crevasse. Since I had no canteen or water bottle, all I could do was to press my face up to the rock and drink my fill.

As late afternoon set in, shadows in the mountains dimmed the light well before sunset and the forest itself diminished it even further. My plan was to walk until I could not see any more. I estimated that I only made about five or six miles that day in a rugged, mostly uphill trek. When the darkness reached the point where all I could make out were the outlines of trees and the ground below me, I could see no detail. As I looked for a good place to hold up for the night, suddenly I heard what sounded like footsteps. I strained my eyes to see but I couldn't make out anything. Could it be an animal? I wondered. There were many deer in these woods, a few bears and even fewer mountain lions. I pulled out the pistol and then just stood still and listened.

The sound of the steps seemed to be intermittent and deliberate, more like human than animal. Could the authorities have dropped police or even troopers in to hunt me down? Maybe I was just being paranoid and acting like a frightened child in the dark. Still, I pushed the switch forward on the weapon and used the laser sight to scan the woods. That sight was the only light I had but unfortunately, it would only illuminate a small area around the target dot. My scan revealed nothing but tree trunks until I looked down. To my horror, there were three laser dots bouncing around on my torso.

"Laser sights come in handy sometimes, don't they? That's why we have 'em too. Drop your weapon." The stern male voice came out of the darkness.

I threw the pistol to the ground and raised my hands. I could only make out the obscure outlines of three figures approaching me. Then one of them turned a bright light on me and shined it right in my face, and then I could see nothing.

"Get down on your knees." He ordered.

I slowly went down on my knees, still not knowing who those people were. But I did realize that they held my life in their hands. One wrong move, or one wrong answer could get me shot dead quickly. My intuition told me by the way they talked and acted, that they were probably not police or military.

"Ok. Now I'm going to ask you some questions. Answer right, more questions, answer wrong, no more questions. Understand?"

"Yes."

"Who are you?"

"My name is Joshua McNeal."

"Joshua, huh. What are you doing here?

Just then one of the men picked up my weapon and brought it to the attention of the questioner.

"Look at his gun."

"Glock 209 Stunner. Standard Police issue. I think I've seen enough."

The man pointed his pistol right at my head and aimed with every intention to fire.

"Wait, it's not my gun!" I cried out expecting the worst.

Then, I heard a woman's voice and footsteps coming out of the darkness.

"What's going on here?" She demanded.

"We captured an infiltrator. He was carrying a Police Glock 209."

The woman walked up to within about six feet of me. Two strong lights were pointed at me, but I could only make out that she had long, full hair and was wearing boots and Army fatigues. She wore a cartridge belt with holster and pistol, and she had a short assault rifle strapped over her front.

"Who are you? What are you doing here?" She shot off her questions in rapid succession.

"My name is Joshua McNeal and I am trying to escape to the Freelands."

"Escape from what? What did you do?"

"I never registered with the I.D.S."

"Then why were you carrying a police pistol?"

"I took it from the officer and then I took his hopper. He was about to arrest me, so I jumped in his hopper and took off."

"Where's the hopper now?"

"You'll find what's left of it and another one that was chasing me at the bottom of the canyon."

"You're not going to buy that, are you?" The third man asked, with a noticeable English accent.

"Are you Americans?" I asked, wanting to know who I was dealing with.

"Americans? That's a strange thing to ask." She said with a hint of surprise in her voice.

"Are you Christians? Militia?" I asked.

"We'll ask the questions for now. Are you a Christian?"

"I really wish I could say I am. I'm Jewish though, well at least half."

"Well I'm full blood Kosher." She said proudly.

"What are we going to do with him?" The man holding the gun on me asked rather impatiently.

"Keep him covered. Get his clothes off, all of them. I'll send Jason down with the scanners. Check every square centimeter of his clothes and every square centimeter of him. And before he puts his pants back on, verify that he is Jewish."

"But it's cold out here."

"We won't inconvenience you for long. If you're not carrying any other weapons or communication devices, and your story checks out, then you can put on your clothes and sleep by a warm fire tonight. But if you're a Government spy or infiltrator, then we'll put a bullet in your head and roll you down the mountain. Will that be alright?"

"That will be fine."

She turned and marched up the hill, disappearing in the darkness. I then began the unpleasant and embarrassing task of disrobing in front of three armed men who I could still not see clearly. When all of my clothes were in a pile, one of the men picked them up one at a time. He felt them for microphones, transmitters, cameras or weapons. I stood there naked and cold when they turned their lights on me. Compliance with their search was humiliating to say the least.

When they were finished with me, they moved back, still with their guns and their lights trained on me. I stood there with my arms folded and shivering for several minutes until I heard someone else come down the hill. From what I could make out as he got closer to me, he was a young man in his late 20's or early 30's, a bit short and stocky, with unkempt shoulder length hair and black, plastic rimmed eyeglasses. He was toting some electronic equipment which he set down on the ground next to me.

"Hi, I'm Jason." He said with a friendly smile as if we were meeting at a social event.

"Hello Jason. I'm Joshua."

"Joshua, I like that name."

"Jason, I wouldn't get too friendly. He may not make it through the night. Just get on with it." The impatient voice came from one of the men who held me at gunpoint.

"Ok, sorry. Now spread your legs apart, hold your arms out and open your mouth." Jason instructed more like a doctor with a patient than a security officer with a suspect.

I complied very willingly to this non-threatening young man. He took out an instrument like a wand attached to a handle. He started from the top of my head and went down and around following the outline of my body. When both sides were scanned, then he went front to back. There was no reaction from him or the instrument.

"Ok, you can put your arms down and stand normally."

Then he spread out each piece of my clothing and waved the wand over them. He picked up my clothes and placed them in front of me.

"You can go ahead and get dressed now. He's clean, nothing in his clothes or on him."

I put my clothes on as rapidly as possible. The night air was getting colder. Being dressed again made it bearable, but it sure would have been nice to have a jacket.

"Am I finished? Did I pass?"

"There is one more thing I'm supposed to check." Jason said as he put down the wand and picked up a portable hand scanner.

He opened a small remote monitor. Somehow this young man was able to hack into the Government data base, not to alter anything, but to search and monitor it.

"Ok Joshua, what is your full name?"

"Joshua Samuel McNeal."

"Please put your hand in the slot and hold still for 30 seconds."

Jason checked his monitor without an expression. I couldn't see the monitor, but past experience told me what was happening.

"He's not in the system." Jason declared as a matter of fact.

"He's not in the system at all?" The question came from one of the guards.

"He's totally not in it, never was."

"Could the police temporarily remove an agent's I.D. from the database?"

"Impossible. Not even the police could do that."

"Thanks Jason. You can pack up your toys now."

"Nice meeting you, Joshua." Jason said to me after he picked up his equipment.

"My pleasure, Jason."

As I heard him lumbering back up the hill, I could not help but feel warmth and friendship for that young man. He might have been what we used to call a nerd, but he did his job without being hardened by it. Just then the lights went off of me. The bright red beams of the laser sights went off and I thought I could hear guns being holstered.

"Sorry to put you through that friend, but we can't be too careful." The guard said in a much welcomed friendlier tone.

"It's alright. I completely understand." I said and I did, once the offense wore off.

I put my clothes back on as fast as I could.

"Just follow Pete back to camp. We'll walk behind."

One of the men directed his light on the trail and started walking up the hill. I followed the light and the silhouette of the man holding it. The other two closed ranks behind me. As we climbed up, we came to a clearing in the trees and the ground just above us seemed to be flat and horizontal. When we got up to it I discovered that it was a paved road, the remains of an old abandoned highway with the painted center line still visible. We followed the road toward a dark mountain which had a glow of yellow light that seemed to come out of the middle of it. The road upon closer examination appeared to have been abandoned for years. The asphalt had wide fissures in it and chunks out of it. And the old highway was covered with rocks and boulders presumably from landslides.

As we got closer to the light source I realized what I was seeing. It was the glow of campfires inside a highway tunnel cored through the mountain. There was a large pile of boulders and rocks obscuring about three quarters of the entrance, leaving only about an eight foot wide opening on one side to enter by. The rock pile may have started as a landslide, but I think that human hands finished the job. Pete stood at the entrance, switched off his light, and invited me in.

I walked in and was amazed to see people spread out on the road from one side to the other and covering the whole length of the tunnel. Small fires were lit and groups of people surrounded each fire. Some were eating, some were sleeping, and some were talking. Upon closer look, there were actually two tunnels which had several yards of open space separating them. There seemed to be about an equal number of people spread out in the far tunnel as well. I estimated there to be something just over 200 people living there.

Finally, I was able to get a good look at the men that held me and nearly executed me. Peter, a black man, was in his mid-thirties, married with two kids living in the camp. He shook my hand after a brief introduction and then went in to join his family. Dennis was a little older than me and was wearing what looked like civilian camping clothes instead of Army surplus. He was originally from England but moved to America as a young man when the British Government abandoned their own people and constitution to become an arm of the One World Government. When the United States followed suit and did the same, he joined the resistance. Alex, the man who was ready to pull the trigger on me was in his late thirties. He wore full Army fatigues and he looked and acted like a soldier, or at least a militiaman. His hair was cut short and he kept his facial hair shaved, which was uncharacteristic of most of the men in the camp. His strong sense of duty stemmed from his desire to protect the people and an intense hatred for the enemy. I sensed that he must have suffered a great loss, but I did not probe. He told me that he still was on watch until 21:00 hours and that the Chief of Security would be in to see me in a few minutes. He shook my hand cordially, and then went back outside.

"Do you suppose that I could get something to eat?" I asked Dennis who was still standing around by the entrance.

"Oh sure, just go up to any of these little groups and tell them you'd like something to eat. It's ok, hunting and forage parties are sent out every day to find food for the camp, so it's all community property you might say."

"I see."

"And when you're ready to go to sleep, just grab an empty blanket or bedroll or ask for one. One thing though, just don't accidentally crawl in with another man's wife. They wouldn't take it too kindly." Dennis said and then laughed at his own joke.

"I'll be careful."

"Ok man, I've got to go. See you around." Then Dennis strolled down to the far end of the tunnel.

I didn't feel comfortable imposing myself on any of the people just yet. Instead, I decided to wait around by the entrance for the Chief of Security, whoever that might be. After several minutes the woman walked into the tunnel. It was the same woman that ordered that I be searched. But I also realized that she was the one who spared my life. She looked to be about my age or a bit older. Her long wavy hair was blown by the wind. She had a plain face which showed a graceful maturity but the sternness of great responsibility. After leaning her rifle against the tunnel wall, she noticed me standing there.

"Joshua, did you get something to eat?"

"No ma'am, not yet."

"Ma'am? I remember hearing that in a real old movie I saw when I was a little girl."

"It's just a term of respect for women where I came from. What should I call you?"

"My name is Sarah. And where do you come from?"

"Well, originally, not too far from here. Just down the hill in Glendale. But that was a very long time ago. I've travelled very far, for many years since then."

"Glendale? You must be older than you look. Is that a wedding ring on your hand?'

"Yes, I was married once. She died a long time ago and I've never found anyone to replace her."

"Children?"

"I had a daughter. She and my wife were both killed in an accident."

"I'm so sorry."

"It was a long time ago."

"Well, you wanted to get to the Freelands. This is it. I don't know what your background is, but this is a hard life. You'll be fighting the elements for survival, and soon you'll be fighting the rest of the world and the Devil himself."

"I want to thank you for taking me in and not rolling my dead body down the mountain. I promise, I won't let you down." She cracked a little smile at my remark.

"We call this Angel Camp."

"Is that because you're all little angels?"

She looked askance at my attempt at humor, so I decided to back off of it for now.

"This used to be called Angeles National Forest."

"Oh yes, I remember. And this road, these tunnels, Angeles Crest Highway! I used to dri… I mean, I've heard about this."

"You're a little odd, but you better get some food while there's some left."

"I'd like to earn my keep. I could stand security watch. I'm pretty good with firearms."

"You'll be assigned a detail in the morning. Maybe we'll start you out with the firewood crew. We need to watch you for a few days before we hand you a firearm."

"Fair enough. Are you the Chief of Security?"

"Things are kind of informal around here. If you do a job, then you can claim the title."

"Thank you Sarah, for everything. Good night."

"Good night."

She turned and went over to a clear spot right up against the tunnel wall. It was an area without many people because it was close to the entrance which allowed more of the cold wind to hit you. I watched her as I moved down the tunnel. She removed her cartridge belt and pistol, spread out a bedroll and sat down on it. She sat all alone, watching the people in the tunnel, glancing over at the entrance like a lioness always on the lookout for threats to her cubs. Sarah was one of the best natural leaders I have ever known.

People were settling in for the night. I walked down the road trying not to step on anyone. Then I heard a woman talk to me from one of the fire circles. She was in a bedroll with her husband who was fast asleep.

"Hello, are you new here?

"Yes. My name is Joshua."

"I'm Joanne. This is my husband Chris. His watch is in a couple hours so he's getting some sleep while he can."

"I see. Well, it's nice to meet you."

"Are you hungry?"

"Yes, as a matter of fact, I am."

"There's some meat left in the pan over there." She pulled out a naked arm from under her blanket and pointed to a covered skillet resting on the pavement next to the dying fire.

"Thank you."

I picked it up by the handle and removed the lid. There were four small pieces of cooked meat left in the pan. I lifted it close to my nose. It had a strange aroma, but I picked up a piece and took a bite. The meat was tough and gamey but it eventually satisfied my hunger.

"We didn't get any venison today."

"What is this?"

"It's either possum or raccoon, I'm not sure which. It takes some getting used to, but you will. There's a blanket over there you can use. Well, good night." She pulled the cover up over her head and turned toward her husband.

"Thanks again." I felt awkward having a conversation with a strange woman who was in bed with her husband in a public place.

I remember having to eat such wild animals in Air Force survival training, so the initial punch of the strange taste was dulled a bit by experience. I must have been very hungry or easily adaptable, for I finished off all the meat in the pan. There were scattered piles of pine needles and leaves lying around. These were used by many as cushions or pillows. They would gather them up, and then lay their blanket down over them. So I made up my bed only a few feet away from Joanne and her husband.

As I lay on the road looking out over the people in the tunnel, I could not help but compare their struggle to the people of London during the Blitz of World War II. When the bombs rained down overhead, they took shelter in the subway tunnels underground. They lived there for days on end and formed communities. But like those people of a century and a half ago, privacy was one of the luxuries lost to them. Men, women and children, all living and working together for their mutual survival. All pride and pretext was stripped away. These people were dedicated to one another for nothing other than the basic business of living. They took me into their community and silently, I thanked God for it. Even then, I knew that God had His hand on me, guiding and protecting me. But I did not know to what end.

CHAPTER 8

SARAH

The days and nights were getting cooler on the mountain and everyone was hoping that the first snowfall would be delayed as long as possible. I was fitting in better than expected with the people of Angel Camp, even getting to know most of them, at least on a casual basis. They made little demand of me, but they shared with me what they had. The camp was like a microcosm of society. Everyone had a job to do. But instead of a government laying down laws or an employer issuing orders, the people would voluntarily take up a task whenever they saw a need. The minor exception to that were the security watches directed by Sarah. Early on, she took on the responsibility of defending the camp and organizing that defense. Sarah had no family living with her. She was intelligent, hardworking and aggressive. When she took on the responsibilities of a leader, she was given the authority of one, however informal that authority may be.

My first days were spent helping to gather firewood. This was a daily task as it was used to cook our food and keep us warm at night. Our forage circles had to spread further and further out because the dead and dry branches that could be picked up on the ground or broken off a tree were getting scarce near the camp. When we found a dead tree in the forest, we would harvest all the limbs off of it and leave only a bare trunk standing. I was happy to work hard for these people and myself, but I still felt that I should have a part in defending the camp also. I could not tell them of my military background because at this time, if you were in the military, you were the enemy. Soon I would bring up the issue with Sarah, but I was giving her time to build up her confidence and trust in me naturally.

When I returned with the firewood crew toting all the wood that I could carry and drag behind me, I rested by the entrance of the eastward tunnel. Near that entrance behind a big stack of wood, Jason had set up his own little electronics workshop. I would often stop by to talk with him. He was preoccupied but always friendly and I think, happy to see me. He had computers, monitors and communication devices organized along the tunnel wall. He was always working on something or monitoring something even as we talked. Solar cells were set up outside to recharge the batteries for all of his equipment. Jason did not do any manual labor or security watches. His job was to keep the camp informed about what was going on with the outside world, but in my opinion, his contributions were worth more than those of any ten men. It was the afternoon but still light. The hunting party was not back yet. Only a few people were in the tunnels. There were classes in Math, Science and the Bible being taught to the younger children. I was so impressed that such advanced culture was being displayed in such primitive conditions.

Somebody told me that tomorrow was Thanksgiving Day. This was a holiday that faded away along with the United States. But the older traditionalists never forgot it and most of the people in the camp continued to honor those holidays that I remember well. Suddenly I heard a shout echoing through from the west tunnel. The hunting party had returned. They nailed seven ducks flying out from the lake. People said it was a miracle, a gift from God for our Thanksgiving Dinner. Although seven ducks would not exactly fill up 230 people, it would be a welcome tasty treat. As the wild game was being rendered for cooking, I helped disperse wood throughout the tunnels and light the evening fires. Because we had no ovens, meat was either roasted over a fire or grilled in a pan. Every effort was made to distribute all of the food equitably.

Every evening Pastor Ron and Pastor Steve would stand in the middle of each tunnel and say a blessing over the food, even as it was cooking over the fires. I didn't know if these men were former Pastors of churches or if they just stepped into that roll to fill a need here in camp. There was no set meal time or bedtime. Several of the men and a few women served as armed sentries on rotating four hour shifts going 24 hours a day, seven days a week. Because of that, people were going in and out at all hours even while most of the people were eating or sleeping. Sarah would stand her own shift on security watch, and then would typically go out and monitor other shifts. But when people like Alex were on watch, she felt freer to spend less time outside and either got some rest herself or just sat there in her solitary space. Sarah was not unfriendly or snobbish. She just did not feel free to socialize or strike up a casual conversation as others did. Sarah was preoccupied, thoughtful and a loner. I recognized the breed.

Thanksgiving morning came and the Pastors led the camp in a praise and worship service which lasted about 30 minutes or so. I witnessed similar things before when I went to church with my wife. But as much as I tried or wanted to, I just could not relate to it or even understand it for myself. I believed in God, but I did not understand Jesus or Yeshua as the Jewish believers called Him. I did not understand how He was relevant to me. There was something bothering me spiritually, something tugging at me, but I didn't know how to deal with it.

Small pieces of last night's duck were distributed through the camp. Since it was the closest thing to turkey that we had, we saved it for a late morning meal. Our vegetable gardens were becoming less productive now that colder weather was setting in. Forage and hunting parties stepped up efforts to bring in food and firewood before the first snowfall, which would make those tasks twice as hard. I was given a worn but warm winter coat by a man in the camp. I was so grateful and I expressed it however inadequately. My dedication and allegiance was to these people and I would do everything in my power to prove it to them.

I looked for an opportunity to talk with Sarah over the next few days. It had to be at a time when both of us were back in the tunnel and not busy. I watched her from time to time, mostly at night and often from a distance. She did not seem to have a personal relationship with any of the other men in the camp. Most of the men were married with their wives and or families living with them. Some were courting the few available ladies, and others were not pursuing intimate relationships at all for a variety of reasons. I had hoped that in the past several days, she had watched me, asked about me and felt more comfortable about me, at least from a security standpoint. That was the approach I decided to take with her. I was determined to prove myself to her more than anybody else in the camp. Although I would never show it or speak of it, I was becoming very attracted to her. I watched her and thought about her constantly. It was as if my feelings were mocking what I perceived myself to be, a self-sufficient loner. But even if the world was about to crash down around us, I wanted and I needed an intimate partner to be with in whatever time we had left. Then one cold and cloudy evening, my opportunity came. Sarah was relaxing up against the tunnel wall. Her assault rifle was leaning against the wall next to her. My work was done for the day, so I walked up to her casually.

"Sarah."

"Hello, Joshua."

"You remembered my name."

"Of course, one of our people's greatest warriors and leaders."

"Our people?"

"You're Jewish aren't you?"

"I guess so. My mother was Jewish."

"Then you're a Jew."

"Ok, and speaking of warriors, I would like to participate in defending the camp. I have experience with weapons and I could stand a security watch, if you feel comfortable with it."

"You know, there's absolutely no Government information on you at all, which tells me that you're not one of them. But we still don't know who you are."

"I've been escaping and hiding, like you, like everyone here."

"How did you do that in the city?"

"I was just passing through the city. Some people helped me, Christian people. I think they took a chance in doing so. I hope everything is alright with them."

"It won't be for long."

"Why haven't they attacked camps like this?"

"There's a twenty year old truce between the new Government and the separatist communities. But that was at a time when we were united, organized and strong. Now, we're disintegrating. Our supplies are being cut off, people abandoning the hard life for the comfort of the city. It's just a matter of time, before they find out how weak we really are."

"Sarah, I want you to know that you can count on me for anything. I'm here to stay as long as you'll have me. I'm through with running away."

"Are you growing a beard?" She asked, turning the conversation to me personally.

I felt the several days' growth on my face, not knowing whether she approved or disapproved.

"I'm sorry, I hadn't thought about shaving. There aren't many mirrors around here you know."

"I think beards look good on men."

"Then, I'll let it grow."

Sarah's smile suddenly turned to a melancholy expression.

"There's really no future in this world for you or me or anyone."

"I thought you're a believer, don't you look forward to the Messiah returning?"

"I am and I do. But the world as we knew it is coming to an end. Soon every believer will be running or fighting for their lives, and many will die. We look for the Lord's return, and that's all we look forward to. So we just wait and endure."

"The end will come when it comes. But I think it's easier to endure suffering and hardship when you're with someone you care about and someone who cares about you. Believe me, I've lived the life of a loner and it makes everything harder, not easier."

"I'm sure that a guy like you can find a much more attractive woman to spend your nights with."

"I haven't seen any yet."

She started laughing and I saw the welcome glimmer in her eye toward me.

"You can relieve Nancy Doogan at 22:00 right here at the west entrance."

"Yes ma'am."

"Will you stop with the ma'am crap? Where did you get that from?" As she asked the rhetorical questions, she gave me a playful punch in the arm.

"See you at 22:00."

"Go on, get out of here." She said while still smiling.

I arrived five minutes early on the road about ten paces outside the tunnel entrance. There was Sarah talking to a woman wearing a cartridge belt and holster which contained a semi-automatic pistol. Nancy Doogan was a single mother with a young teenage son. She seemed to be a strong and responsible woman as I found most of the women in the camp to be. Sarah made the introduction. Nancy handed over the cartridge belt. I adjusted it and put it on. After I checked the magazine on the weapon and verified that a round was in the chamber, I holstered it and took the light from her. I walked around outside of the tunnel pacing back and forth in about a 20 yard radius circle. The night was dark and cold and as I walked and watched, I could not help but admire the strength and discipline of these civilians. In the military, we were trained to do such things and it is almost always a lonely, boring chore.

In the next several days I stood nightly watches and one day Sarah had me team up with Alex for a daytime patrol. Alex had a hard crust on him as far as first impressions go. But in talking with him, I realized that it was mostly on the surface and in time, I think we understood each other. Maybe we could become friends I thought, or at least as much as two soldiers thrown together in war can be friends. My contact with Sarah had been brief, either strictly business or casual and superficial. That situation was becoming intolerable for me. I missed the time we spent together talking several nights ago. When we would look at each other or talk briefly, I could see an interest in her eyes, but work, or the lack of privacy, or maybe even fear kept our relationship from advancing to the level that I wanted it to go.

I saw my opportunity one morning as I was heading out to join the foraging crew. There was Sarah walking by herself in the forest. On this occasion, she was not armed because the weapons had to be used by the day patrols, security watches and the hunting parties. I walked toward her and called out her name before she heard me or saw me approach because I did not want her to think that I was sneaking up on her.

"Sarah."

"Joshua, what are you doing here?"

"I need to discuss something very important with you."

"What is it?"

"Can we step behind that boulder for a minute? It's kind of private."

"Nothing in this camp is private."

"This is… Please." I motioned for her to walk a few feet with me behind a large granite rock which would put a visual barrier between us and the tunnels.

She looked at me strangely, but walked over with me.

"What is it?"

"Something has been bothering me for a while."

"What?

"I am concerned that it has been too long since you've been properly kissed."

She snickered with surprise and then sort of turned her head away, shaking it in disbelief.

"I suppose that you want to try and rectify that situation."

"I think that it is part of my duty and responsibility to this camp."

She stood still looking at me with welcoming eyes. I slowly placed my hands between her cheeks and her long wavy hair. My hands came together at the back of her head as I used my thumbs to pin her hair back. I pulled her slowly toward me until our lips met, gently and briefly at first and then over and over with excitement and passion that we both were caught up in for a few blissful moments. We separated and she just stood there looking at me without saying a word.

"Now remember what we discussed." I said as I left her there, a bit off balance.

After that, Sarah and I no longer felt the need to conceal the affection that we had for one another. There was one exception. A serious security meeting was held after Jason had monitored a news broadcast. He had recorded the event although it was running live all day. Sarah, Alex, Dennis and the two pastors were huddled in the back of the tunnel watching the playback. I walked over and Sarah allowed me to participate.

In essence the big news was that Sheyer wanted to reach out to all of the Separatist and Christian communities around the world and bring them into the fold so to speak. The New Era had brought all of the nations in line, but not all of the people. That uneasy peace had been a thorn in the side of Governments for years. Sheyer, along with the World Council proposed an amnesty to all people living outside the economic and political system if they would voluntarily comply within six months. No mention was made about what would happen to those who did not comply. So again, Sheyer was lauded as the great leader and problem solver of our time. The reporters kept saying that he was extending the olive branch to his enemies for the sake of unity. When Jason turned the monitor off, the quiet discussion began.

"What do you make of that?" Dennis asked of the group.

"We all thought that Sheyer would be the one, but now he's reaching out to us. Maybe we were wrong." Pastor Steve suggested to the surprise of the others.

"It's a trap. He's just trying to thin us out at the same time gather intel on us from the defectors." Alex argued strongly.

"I agree with Alex." Sarah said.

"But what if you're wrong? There are millions of Christians already living in the system and outside the system. Shouldn't they have the right to choose?" Pastor Steve replied in a manner that left the others guessing whether that was what he really believed or if he was just playing devil's advocate.

"There is no way that we can allow this. What are we going to do, call up the Government and have them fly out a police transport to come and pick them up?" Sarah argued.

"With all due respect to my brother Steve, I think we should wait and see. This could be a trap, or it could be a legitimate offer. We should keep this to ourselves for now and just monitor the situation." Pastor Ron weighed in.

"Sheyer can't be trusted. You never know what he's going to do next." Dennis added.

"He knows exactly what he's doing. It's called divide and conquer. First, you offer a solution, and then you create dissention and division among your enemy. Those who cling to their independence will be made to look like villains for bringing trouble on everybody. When the enemy is weak and divided, then they will be isolated and eventually, attacked." I spoke up not being able to hold my peace.

"How do you know all this?" Pastor Steve asked.

"History, it's more less the playbook of every tyrant who ever lived." I answered unapologetically.

"I say for now, we keep this news to ourselves. Are we all agreed?" Sarah spoke up trying to reach a resolution.

The whole group, even Pastor Steve agreed to keep the news from the others in the camp, at least for a while.

That night, I picked the most open spot in the tunnel to lay out my bedroll. To my surprise and delight, Sarah walked over and sat down next to me.

"Do you want some company?"

"Absolutely."

"I can't spend the night here."

"I understand."

"I liked what you had to say today. You seem to know a lot about different things for a man on the run most of your life."

"People often surprise us, once you get to know them."

"I guess so."

"What about you? What made you run?"

"I was a wife and a mother with two kids, a boy 9 and a girl 7. My husband made a good living as a regulatory attorney for the North American League. We had everything we needed materially. But something was troubling me in my spirit. I looked at the world around me and how wrong things were. People were mocking and abusing Christians, denying them their rights and forcing many to live apart from our great progressive society. The Christians worshipped a Jew and they used our sacred scriptures. I had to look into it for myself. There was a small Messianic Temple on the west side of the city. I went in and talked to the Rabbi there. He showed me Messiah in the prophets, Isaiah and elsewhere. It was Yeshua, Jesus. Not only that Jesus was our Messiah, but that He died for our sins to make us right with God and to give us eternal life. I devoted my life to following the Lord from that day. Eventually, I tried to share the Lord with my family, but my husband would have none of it. I continued to teach my children about Jesus. When my husband found out, he took our children away and got a court order forbidding me to get near them. Well, I don't give up that easy. I finally tracked them down and when I insisted on seeing my children, he had me arrested. I spent 30 days in jail and in that time, I was served with a summary writ of divorce and I was not allowed to know where my children were living. I never saw them again. It was shortly after that when I realized that Christians need to get tough or die. I took a day trip with a women's group into the foothills before they built the fence. I broke away from the group and hiked up the mountain until I found a Christian colony living up here, some of those became Angel Camp."

"Then Jesus is more important to you than anyone else."

"Yes, He is."

"You know, you are the third woman in my life who's tried to tell me that, maybe now, it's time for me to listen."

"What do you mean?"

"I mean that it is a powerful force that causes people to reject comfort and safety to follow an idea. The law of action and reaction is undeniable in the universe. I've seen the reaction, now I want to discover the action behind it. I mean to discover God and what He wants from me."

"I'm very glad to hear you say that."

"I'll be leaving tomorrow morning."

"Leaving? Why? For where?"

"Mount Wilson"

"Why? There's nothing up there but an old abandoned observatory and some broken down transmitter towers."

"But it's a mountain top, and I'm a Jew. I have to find God on a mountain top."

"Are you crazy?"

"Maybe, but it's what I have to do. I don't know, maybe by getting away from the distractions of life and even people for a while, I can hear God."

"Joshua, you don't have to climb a mountain to find God."

"I'll be leaving before dawn, and I won't be back until I've found what I'm looking for."

"I pray you find it." She said with sadness as she stood up and went back to her own space.

The sky was showing its first sign of light as I got my bedroll and gear together for my trip. There was a diminishing store of pre-packaged; freeze dried emergency rations for the camp. Sarah allowed me to take only a water canteen, two days' rations and no weapons except for a knife. I think she stayed up to see me off but she was obviously upset about my leaving to settle this issue. But I did stop to see her again before I headed down the road. I wanted to kiss her, but there were people around. I could see in her eyes that look of self-defense against a coming rejection, but I did not know how to convince her that it was not the case.

"Will we see you again?"

"Yes. But after I figure out what God wants from me."

"Well, just in case He decides not to speak to you from a burning bush, let me give you something." She reached down and grabbed a book from her bedroll.

"What's this?"

"It's called a Bible. It's God's word, and in it, you'll find out what He wants from you, which is the same thing that He wants from all of us. Anyway, here it is. This is where it is. It's where it's always been." She handed it to me with a hint of a watery eye that she tried to hold back.

"Thank you, Sarah. I'll be back."

"Just find your Lord and Savior Joshua, that's the most important thing."

"Good bye." With that, I turned out onto the dark road.

Sunrise comes late and sunset comes early in the forest. But the sky was light enough for me to see the road ahead. I followed the old highway for several hours until I reached the narrow road that meandered southward through the mountains and terminated by the old observatory. The roads on which I walked were long since rendered impassable by normal street vehicles. Earthquakes, landslides, weather and neglect have turned these once scenic routes into barely adequate foot trails. Still, I was enjoying the walk, the mountains and the forests. The sun was shining brightly through scattered clouds and the air was cool, fresh and exhilarating.

I was told that the observatory and all of the old transmission stations were closed and abandoned several decades ago. Since then, squatters of all kinds and even Christian colonies have occupied what was left of the buildings and even the empty shell of the observatory dome. But in recent years, the Government was sending surveillance drones around the site and aircraft overhead to monitor the people encamped there. Eventually, it was decided that the top of Mount Wilson was too conspicuous and indefensible for the people to remain there. I did not know who or what I would find there as I rounded the curve and saw the cluster of transmission towers, most of which were still standing in the golden afternoon sun.

The buildings that remained were thoroughly picked over for anything that could be of use. Many were constructed of sheet metal over a simple frame. But as I searched for adequate shelter, I noticed that any part of a building that was made of wood was gone whether it was on the outside or inside. So I would have to scrounge the forest for firewood because not a stick of wood remained in any building. I decided to make camp in the big, empty, observatory dome and build my fire in the middle of the concrete floor.

The purpose of my coming to this place had returned to the forefront of my mind. I walked a short distance carrying only Sarah's Bible in my hand. I looked out to the south and saw a clear view of the great city sprawled out below me and the Pacific Ocean beyond. There was about an hour of daylight left and a cold breeze was blowing. I sat down on a stone wall with my back to the wind and I opened the Bible.

When I had read the Bible in the past, much of it seemed confusing and meaningless to me. But now that I was truly seeking answers and direction, every verse I read spoke to me clearly, like a light being switched on. It became compelling to me to discover how God deals with people in different circumstances. I couldn't put it down. People of faith suffered loss and hardship. They were confused and even strayed away like me. But when they returned to God, they always found help and forgiveness. I sensed God's hand helping me to get this far, but I was realizing that I also have offended Him and was in need of forgiveness.

I was so engrossed in reading that I was not paying attention to how dark it was getting. Putting my finger in the page, I closed the book and went into the empty steel building. The large telescope and all of the operating systems had long since been removed leaving only a massive empty shell. I lit my fire in the middle of the circular pit where the base of the telescope once rested. The light of the fire flickered eerily on the great dome ceiling. I could not help but be impressed by what the people of my country constructed almost 200 years ago to expand their understanding of the universe. But looking back to things long gone is not what I needed to do.

Reading by the firelight became distracting and tiring, so after about an hour I closed the book and wrapped myself up in my bedroll. As I lay there looking up into the dome, I wondered if God would speak to me, but at some point, I couldn't tell how long, I fell asleep.

The old observatory had fallen into disrepair and had ceased to be a light tight structure a long time ago. Daylight was filtering in through the holes and cracks. The last smoldering embers of my fire were dying out. I felt as if I were in a giant freezer. My breath fogged out in front of my face. I rushed to the door to relieve myself outside. To my surprise, I saw snow on the ground and on the trees and buildings. A light snowfall had dusted the mountain top during the night. The steel towers were white and covered with ice and looked other worldly. But the sun was out and there were only a few scattered clouds in the sky. I knew that unless the weather changed, most of the snow would be gone by the afternoon.

I took the Bible and sat near the open door. I looked over the chapter headings to read more thoroughly all of text that was interesting to me. When I got to the New Testament, I found myself no longer skimming through it, but reading every word. My eyes were opening as I read. Jesus was much more than a wise man or prophet. He was God on Earth, in human flesh. No one else could ever do the things He did, the ultimate of which was to raise Himself from the dead and then to appear and speak to many of the people who knew Him. The Bible says that He will return to Earth again to establish His kingdom of justice and righteousness.

So much of the New Testament speaks about future events, the end times, which is what I imagined myself to be in. I could read in sobering detail, the events leading to the end, the events that have already taken place and those things which will shortly come about. The Bible is true, about the past, the present and the future. It is there to instruct us, warn us and encourage us.

What I concluded was that the Bible lays out the whole drama of the human race from their beginning to their ultimate destiny. And that there has only ever been two camps among humans, those who follow God, and those who do not. I began to see that even though the people who refuse to follow God are more numerous and more powerful, they have no future, they are lost, and no matter the price, I was not going to be among them.

When I turned back to John 3:16, I could go no further. It spoke right to my heart and at that moment I sought God's grace and forgiveness. I stood in the doorway looking out at the trees and sky. I asked the Lord Jesus to forgive me, to come into my life and make me His own. That was a commitment that I would never turn back on.

My mental processes remained about the same. My body still made demands of me and complained when those demands were not met. Yet the hopelessness and despair in my soul was gone. I was now part of a family, joining all Christians everywhere in help and solidarity. All of us eagerly awaiting the return of our Lord.

There was no longer any need for me to remain on the mountain. I scooped up some clean slush and stuffed it into my canteen until it was full. It would be a vigorous walk back, but I figured that I could still make Angel Camp before dark. I set out on my return trip, thinking about my new life, thinking about my friends, and thinking about Sarah.

The sun was still illuminating the sky as I arrived at Angel Camp. When I got within sight of the west tunnel entrance, I saw Sarah herself standing security watch. She heard and saw me approach, raising her gun in my direction, and then she recognized me. She lowered her weapon and walked toward me as I walked toward her.

"Joshua, did you find what you were looking for?"

"I found my Savior, the Lord Jesus. I guess He had to run me through the ringer to get me to finally seek Him. But I found Him, and I'm never going back. And God willing, I'll never leave you again."

Sarah dropped her rifle and wrapped her arms tightly around me, burying her head in my chest. I touched the back of her head, not knowing whether she was laughing, crying or praying. When she lifted up her head and looked at me, her eyes were full of tears. She just stared into my eyes.

"I love you, Joshua."

"I love you too, Sarah."

We then kissed and held each other as tightly as we could. Our lips pressed together hard and our heads and hands moved freely over each other.

"Maybe we should get a room." I quipped after a moment of separation.

"Maybe we should get married."

"I'd love to. But how can we do that?"

"We have two ordained ministers in the camp."

"Yes, that's true. Alright my love, we'll be married."

"And I want it to be a Jewish wedding."

"Anything you say."

We kissed again as passionately as before.

"Let me take your watch, you go in and make arrangements."

"You must be tired, why don't you just go inside and rest for now."

"I'd rather not walk in there just yet if it's all the same with you."

She smiled at me, handed me her rifle and strolled into the tunnel.

The whole camp seemed to rejoice for Sarah and me and many contributed to making the ceremony special for us. Weddings have been performed before in these remote camps but by necessity they have mostly been short and simple affairs. But because Sarah was so loved and respected in the camp, people went the extra mile to make her day memorable. I had made several friends myself. I asked

Jason, who I found out was half Jewish like me, to stand with me. And I asked the hardnosed soldier, Alex to stand with me as well.

A Chuppah or canopy was erected in the forest, just off the old highway. They had found and trimmed four pine branches, each about eight feet long to serve as poles for the canopy. The cover was a large, light colored blanket. The weather had become unseasonably warm and dry in these early days of December, a condition not unheard of in Southern California. It seemed that all things were working out to bless our day.

Morning came and I found myself surrounded by many of the men in the camp. Sarah was off somewhere out of sight being attended to by many of the women of the camp. We had been separated since the day before. I was given a white robe made from an unused sheet which draped over my clothes and a round, flat cap for my head. The men led me out to the canopy where others from the camp were gathered around. Pastor Ron and Pastor Steve were standing on the far side of the canopy as we approached. All of the men wore head coverings of one kind or another, even if crudely improvised. When I reached the canopy, the men circled it and joined the other witnesses. Jason and Alex stood behind me.

Through the woods we could see and hear the bridal procession approaching. I saw what must have been Sarah in a beautiful blue gown, obviously borrowed from one of the ladies in the camp. Sarah had a white veil over her head and was being led by two single file lines of women, one on her right and one on her left. Since I have never seen Sarah in anything other than heavy Army Surplus, seeing her wonderful feminine shape and legs through the gown made me all the more grateful and excited to be there. Sarah came up to the canopy as the other women joined the group of witnesses. Two women stood behind her.

Jason and Alex gently positioned me to the center of the canopy, and then they withdrew. Sarah then slowly began to walk around me. Her veil was still down, but I could see her smiling as she walked.

She made seven circles around me and then stopped and stood next to me. Pastor Ron then opened up the Ketubah.

"I hold in my hand the Ketubah or Wedding Contract signed by Joshua for his commitment to Sarah as her husband and to fulfill all of his marital obligations to her. I will now read the terms of the contract aloud so that Joshua may reaffirm each term in the presence of God and this assembly. Joshua McNeal, do you promise to take Sarah Levin as your one and only wife as long as you both shall live?"

"I do promise."

"Joshua, do you promise to provide food and clothing, shelter and protection to Sarah to the best of your ability?"

"I do promise."

"Joshua, do you promise to satisfy Sarah's needs both physical and emotional and to seek to satisfy her before yourself?"

"I do promise."

"Joshua, do you promise to make your body available to your wife as she requires it except for times of illness or necessary separation?

"I do enthusiastically promise." Some of the witnesses and even the Pastor chuckled.

"And finally Joshua, do you promise to remain faithful to Sarah, forsaking all others as long as you both shall live?"

"I do promise."

"Will the two witnesses now sign the contract that the groom has pledged himself to?"

Jason and Alex stepped up to sign the contract.

"Sarah, in return for Joshua's commitment to you, will you promise before God and this assembly to be a wife, a companion and a helper to him as long as you both shall live?"

"I do promise."

"Sarah, do you promise to be willing to bare and raise children between you both and maintain the household?"

"I do promise."

"And finally Sarah, do you promise to remain faithful to Joshua, forsaking all others as long as you both shall live?"

"I do promise."

Then a woman poured some wine into a glass and handed it to Pastor Steve.

"Wine symbolizes the joy of married life of which you are both about to partake."

Pastor Steve handed me the glass and I took a drink. Sarah lifted her veil and I handed her the glass. She took a drink.

"Does the groom have anything to offer the bride as a symbol of his pledge?"

"I have a ring."

I think Sarah was surprised to see that I had taken my wedding band off and presented it to her. I placed it on her finger and then recited the traditional vow.

"Behold, you are consecrated to me with this ring according to the Law of Moses and Israel."

"And now by the authority of our Lord and Savior, Yeshua King of Israel and King of Kings, I now pronounce you husband and wife. You may kiss the bride."

I kissed my wife and suddenly felt more whole than I had in years. Pastor Steve handed back the wine glass and I gave it to Sarah. She took a drink and then handed it back to me. I finished it off, and then dropped it to the ground where I smashed it under my foot. Suddenly, the whole camp started clapping and cheering. "Mazel Tov" could be heard from many in the crowd. We celebrated until dark, some formed circles and danced the Hora, but it was mostly eating and intimate conversations with friends that were like family.

After dark when people were starting to head back to the tunnels for the night, I was talking to some people and eventually lost track of Sarah. I asked about her and a woman pointed me to a narrow trail through the woods. She told me that I would find her at the end of the trail and then she handed me a light. I turned the light on and followed the trail for about 75 yards until I saw a tent. It was a light, four person camping tent, one of several that we had stocked. I poked through the opening and saw Sarah in a double sleeping bag. I turned the light off her face and set it down to give a low, indirect light in the tent. Sarah's hair was down around her as her head rested on the air pillow. The cover was up to her neck, but one bare arm was outside.

"Excuse me mam, but I was just looking for a place to get warm."

"It's warm in here."

"Are you married?"

"Yes."

"When will your husband be back?"

"He should be along anytime."

"Will he mind if I get in the sack with you?"

"No, I don't think he'll mind."

I started to lift the cover when she stopped me.

"Your clothes, I don't allow men to get into my bed with their clothes on."

"Sorry, I didn't mean to be inconsiderate."

I threw off my clothes as fast as I could and then crawled in next to her. Her soft, warm body made me remember that this was about as close to Heaven as it gets on this Earth. I rolled on top of her and looked her in the eye.

"So, do you wanna smack?"

She laughed right in my face. I was a bit taken aback by that reaction, but she brought me back.

"It's been a long time since I've had a good smacking. And you look like just the man that can do it."

And so we pleasured each other non-stop and without limit, all through the night. For a few blissful hours, we had forgotten the world around us.

CHAPTER 9

UNHOLY WAR

For the next several days things were quiet in Angel Camp. Life was still a struggle, especially with winter on the horizon. There was plenty of hard work and precious little privacy. But being with the one you love can make any place feel like home. Sarah and I were happy together and I took every opportunity I could to spend time with her and to bring her whatever pleasure that was in my power. I also grew closer to the people. Some had become close friends, but I could not help feeling love and respect for them all. These were real people, weak, flawed, and vulnerable as everyone but together we were a family. Love and charity were in their hearts, responsibility and duty were in their minds. Nobody had to be forced to do what was right.

One late afternoon I was returning to the tunnel with a large bundle of firewood that I was dragging behind me on a rope. I heard a commotion inside, so I dropped the rope and went inside to see what was going on. People were gathered around Jason who had picked up a big story on World Net News. Sarah was there, but I could not get close enough to see for myself. A couple of the guys were yelling back to the crowd with the main points of the story.

"Sheyer's been shot!" One man yelled. Then some in the crowd cheered.

"Is he dead? Who shot him?" Questions came from the back of the crowd.

"He's not dead yet, but he was shot in the head. They don't give him much chance." The answer came.

Jason turned up the volume so many more could hear the story for themselves at it was being repeated over and over throughout the night. Many in the camp were relieved to hear the news because of Sheyer's previous anti-Christian rhetoric. But Sarah, me and a few others had a bad feeling about it. Not that anyone had any sympathy for Sheyer, but we waited to see what the World Council's reaction would be and who would be blamed.

Most of the camp spent the night huddled around Jason's satellite receiver instead of their usual fire circles. Sheyer was barely holding on to life as he lay in a hospital in Rome where he was speaking earlier. A high powered rifle was used to do the deed and the search for the perpetrator went on. There was anger and concern expressed from all over the world but the anger came to a head and our worst fears were realized when it was announced that a suspect had been arrested, and that he had links to a Christian terrorist group. Rightly or wrongly, Christians would be blamed for the attempted assassination of the most popular world leader ever.

Until Sheyer came along, the Council was mostly content to let the status quo prevail when it came to the Christians and the Anti-Government Separatists. But Sheyer insisted on the complete participation and unity of every person on the planet, and his first move toward that was the amnesty deal. As the night went on, we heard interviews with everyone from high ranking politicians to the person on the street. Whether it was all orchestrated or real, the overriding consensus seemed to have been that the Christian communities have been given enough special privileges and it was time to start reeling them in.

The crowd thinned out considerably around the satellite receiver until only a few diehards kept vigil into the early morning hours. Even Sarah and I went over to our secluded spot and laid there holding each other, thinking about what might happen next. There was a tension in the air which made everyone's sleep less easy.

When I woke up as the first light of dawn filtered into the tunnel, I noticed a stunned look on the faces of those that were still monitoring the events. Sarah was still asleep, but I had to go over and find out what was happening.

"What is it? What's happening?" I asked to anyone who would answer me.

"He's recovered. Sheyer has completely recovered. They're calling it a miracle." A woman told me, hardly believing it herself as she was saying it.

"What do you mean he's completely recovered? You mean he's out of danger, off the critical list?" I asked wanting more clarification.

"No, I mean he's walking around and talking to the press as if it never happened." She answered emphatically.

"Unbelievable." I muttered.

It was hard for everyone to get about their daily work because of the anxiety of what would happen next. The batteries powering the receiver were running low because we had been monitoring it all night long. Jason had a spare set of batteries on the solar chargers outside, but it was a dark, overcast day and it would take all day for them to fully charge. We decided to give it a rest for a few hours to save the batteries and also because there was nothing we could do about it anyway. But when Jason switched back on in the afternoon, he would report any new developments.

Sarah woke up and I went over to give her a kiss before I started my shift on security watch. I was assigned to patrol with Alex in the forest surrounding the camp. We didn't talk much on patrol because we were supposed to watch and listen. But Alex and I got to know each other and understand each other over the past several days.

Sarah decided to add to the watches after the assassination attempt on Sheyer. But Sarah was right about the weakened condition of the Christian communities. Only a handful of people in Angel Camp could remotely pass for a soldier. And in the back of everyone's mind was the expectation that we would all be forced to become soldiers.

In the midafternoon, runners were sent out to call back the forage parties, the hunting parties and even the security patrols for an emergency meeting. We all filtered back into the tunnels and risked the short term lack of sentries for the sake of a discussion which must include the whole camp. Sarah stood up to address the entire camp, which is something that she typically did not do.

"About two hours ago, we received a newscast of a resolution from the World Council, changing the status of the delegates to that of deputies, effectively giving Sheyer dictatorial power over the Council. Now this was done after a former Cardinal from the Vatican, who now calls himself the "Prophet", proclaimed that Sheyer is the one that all of the religions of the world have been waiting for. This "Prophet" claims that Sheyer is the fifth incarnation of Buddha, the Islamic Mahdi, the Jewish Messiah, and the second coming of Christ. But what's more frightening is that this Prophet was able to produce fire in the sky which appeared to come out of nowhere and hovered over the ground for a few minutes."

"It's an aerial hologram." A man from the crowd yelled out.

Sarah turned to Jason, who reluctantly spoke out to address that issue.

"This apparently happened in full daylight, and the fire stream was more than five miles high. There is no holographic projector on Earth that can overcome the ambient daylight and project a clear, solid looking image over that much space."

"Not only that, but many people who were there claimed to have felt the heat from the fire. And it was recorded on video and broadcast all over the world. It couldn't have been just an image." Pastor Ron added.

"Well, what does this all mean?" A young mother asked with anxiety in her voice.

"I'm afraid that this is Biblical prophecy coming true. Wouldn't you agree, Pastor Ron?" Sarah asked.

"I think it's undeniable." Pastor Ron answered solemnly.

"This means that they're coming after Christians, because we're the only ones left who know that he is an imposter empowered by Satan. So war is coming people and we better be ready for it." Sarah answered.

"How can we be ready for it? How can we possibly win? A middle aged man asked.

Sarah thought for a moment before answering.

"We can't win. But we can choose how we will live and how we will die. For myself, I prefer to go down fighting the enemies of God and of our people. I'm not saying that they'll get all of us. We will keep undercover as best we can until the Lord returns. We won't look for a fight, but if they come after us, we'll fight." Sarah proclaimed defiantly.

I stood there and listened to my wife with such pride in my heart. She reminded me of Patrick Henry and others from American history, who stood their ground in the face of impossible odds. I would support my wife in every way.

So for the next several days, Angel Camp was on high alert. Armed watches were only assigned to those who would not hesitate to shoot if they saw an armed intruder. People were told that if police or soldiers caught them away from camp, they were not to run toward camp, but to fight or run away from camp. The consensus was that if they were captured and arrested, they would eventually be made to talk.

Meanwhile, many of us were monitoring the news over the satellite receiver. Christians were indeed blamed for the assassination attempt on Sheyer. The so-called Prophet was convincing the world that Christians were the scourge of humanity and the last living obstacle to progress and unity. Sheyer had already begun to send his legions against Christian communities around the world. In Middle America, The South American League, The African Federation, The South Pacific League, large Christian towns and cities were being surrounded by troops, armored vehicles, artillery and aircraft. In each case the community was given the opportunity to surrender. Some did and were moved to re-education camps. But most of the people fought the invasion. The Christians fought valiantly with what they had, but within a few weeks they were all overrun. Sarah was right. Christians were not ready for this fight. They were outnumbered and outgunned. And they were hated throughout the whole world.

The first dreaded winter storm finally fell on the mountain three days before Christmas. The celebration of the holiday would be much different than it had been in the past. Instead of multiple fire circles in the tunnels at night, only one fire would be allowed in the middle of each tunnel to reduce our heat signature that would be picked up with infrared sensors in satellites and aircraft. Although human beings can be picked up on infrared if they are outside of the tunnel, it would be unlikely that the Government would launch a military operation if they believed that there were only a few people in hiding.

Christmas was celebrated with prayer, a short sermon from each Pastor and testimonies of encouragement from various people as we all came closer together around two small fires. And as we all tried to get closer to God, we were all waiting for the other shoe to drop from the one that everyone was now calling Anti-Christ. The tension in the air had changed our daily lives and desires as often happen to people in times of war or great distress. Appetites for enjoying food and even lovemaking decline to very low priorities. Sarah and I just lie together holding each other and express our love for each other on a much deeper level.

The snow and the constant search for surveillance aircraft and drones made life more difficult, but human beings are incredibly adaptable when they have to be. As the first few weeks of the New Year unfolded, the difficulties of the cold weather and the extra vigilance all became a matter of routine again. But that routine would once again shift when Jason picked up a radio message, not from the media, but from the Wrightwood Camp.

Military transports had landed on the old highway on both ends of the town. Leaflets were dropped from the air, demanding their surrender. The call was desperate. The town was going to put up a fight, but called out to the surrounding communities for whatever assistance they could give. Wrightwood was about 20 miles to the east, which would be a half day march for the most seasoned soldier. Angel Camp was not in a position to render assistance, but I believe that they would if they could have.

Sarah and most of the leadership of the camp listened intently to the shortwave broadcast on a set that Jason had cobbled together from spare parts. We dared not respond because we did not want to give ourselves away. It was about two hours after the message was first intercepted that we began to hear that the Government forces had opened fire on the town. The intelligence that we had about Wrightwood was that there were about 1500 people living there, including women and children. But we did not know exactly how many fighters they had or how well they were armed.

As word got out around the camp about the Wrightwood situation, everyone was very much on edge. That battle was taking place only 20 miles away which was nothing when you consider that the Government was using flying troop transports. Then at last, the transmission ended. The dreaded silence came. The town was being destroyed and its residents were being killed. It didn't take a lot of imagination to realize how it would all end.

The day that we had all dreaded was upon us. Sarah called a security meeting. Everyone was to pack up and be prepared for immediate evacuation. An inventory was made of all the weapons in the camp. There were 28 long guns, which included 18 assault rifles, 6 shotguns, and 4 hunting and sniper rifles. There were also 32 handguns, mostly of the semi-automatic type. Sarah dispensed the weapons to the men and women most capable and willing to use them effectively. There would be no fires and no hot meals that night.

Nobody wanted to sleep that night. We tried to keep the worst of the news and speculative talk away from the hearing of the younger children. Angel Camp was armed and on a war footing, but the armed sentries were ordered to sleep in shifts with their weapons at their side.

"We can't stay here." Sarah whispered to me.

"I know. There are too many kids and older people. We'll move too slow." I whispered back.

"That's the way it is. What can we do?" She asked me in a rare moment of vulnerability.

"We're all in God's hands. We have to try and hold on until He returns." I answered in all sincerity, but still surprised finding myself preaching to Sarah.

"They trusted me to organize things and to protect them." She confided.

"And you have. You've done an amazing job, darling. Nobody can stop what's happening. It's happening to all of us."

"I know and love every one of these people. I saw them join us little by little as families or small groups until we became a community."

"Small groups?" I asked as her words gave me an idea.

"Yes, mostly. Some came individually like you and me." She added.

"Small groups, that's it!" I declared.

"What's it?"

"Angel Camp has to break up into small groups. Groups of 10 to 15 people going in 20 different directions. Only in that way do some of us have a chance to survive."

"But how can we fight them if we're all separated into small groups?"

"We don't fight them. We can't fight them. We run, we hide, we forage and we survive."

"It means saying goodbye to most of our friends, not knowing what will happen to them." She answered sadly.

"I know. War does that. But they will have the best chance to survive. A small group can hide more effectively than a large one. Can you imagine 230 people walking down the highway? They'll spot us and pick us off before you know it. But if we're all going in different directions, it will be harder, and they'll have less incentive to go after small groups in hiding."

"I suppose you're right. We'll have a meeting and break up into groups at first light. I love you."

I kissed my wife tenderly then I went outside to join the night watch.

But as dawn broke, it was the early morning watch which noticed the large plume of black smoke rising up from the east. An alarm was sounded in the camp and everyone was rousted up to our final emergency meeting. Sarah had already discussed our plans with the Pastors and other leaders of the camp. They all reluctantly agreed that it was the right thing to do.

Families would remain together. Each group would have in it at least two "soldiers" who were heavily armed. The freeze-dried and other long lasting rations were distributed evenly. Everyone except the young children would carry their bedrolls and tents on their backs. It was decided that the groups with small children must leave immediately to put as much distance between themselves and the advancing Government troops as possible.

It was difficult to say goodbye to friends and to send vulnerable people out into the wilderness to fend for themselves. There was little time for ceremony. We prayed for each other, exchanged many hugs and shed a few tears, but then they were on their way, one group after another. The soldiers in each group were to decide the direction and destination of the group only well after leaving camp. They were not to discuss it before. Some would choose to stay in the mountains. That would be easier to hide in but harder to live in, especially in the winter. Other alternatives would be to cross over the mountains to the north into the High Desert Plateau, a mostly rural area with several small towns. Another option would be eastward into the less populated San Gabriel and Inland Valleys.

We watched as the groups walked out of sight. Some went up the mountain, some went down the mountain others walked westward alone the old highway. One stalwart group walked eastward on the highway, right toward the enemy's last known position. After everyone had gone, there were just 12 of us left standing by the tunnel entrance keeping watch in the morning sky for Government troop transports. Sarah carried her fully automatic assault rifle, which is the only rifle that our group had. They gave me back the Glock 209 handgun that I brought with me. Alex and Peter were with us and they each carried a semi-automatic handgun. Those were all the firearms that our group was left with.

No sooner had we finished helping each other pack up than we all heard the low roar from the sky. We didn't see anything at first because we were mainly looking east. But the roar got louder and we saw them coming not from the east, but from the north, over the ridgeline and hidden by the mountain and the forest until they were upon us. Suddenly, about a dozen troop transports filled the sky over the tunnels. These aircraft were flat, rectangular shaped vehicles which were powered by hydrogen gas jets like the hoppers. They could take off and land vertically or hover. Each one could carry up to 24 troops along with light artillery and other equipment. They were typically painted flat grey or camouflage. They were hovering right over our position. We could feel the heat from the engines and the noise became deafening.

"Let's go!" I shouted.

"Which way?" Peter shouted back.

"Down." I yelled and then darted out of the tunnel and off the edge of the road.

Everyone followed me down the slope. We had to let the slower, unarmed people get ahead so we who were armed could cover their escape. The transports set down along the highway on both sides of the tunnels. Then we could hear the gangway doors open and the troops run out. Some of the troopers looked over the side to try and spot us. Then a few headed down the slope after us. Sarah stopped and took cover behind a tree. I wanted us to keep moving. I yelled to her, but she popped out from behind the tree with her gun blazing on full automatic.

"Sarah!" I yelled, but she didn't hear me.

She got two of them and they slid down the slope past us. Alex and I also opened fire and the troopers retreated back up to the highway. They were still firing on us from the highway, but with no effect. We knew the mountain and the best path down the slope, anyone else might slide down all the way to the bottom of the canyon. Although I didn't want Sarah taking chances like that, she did stop the troopers from coming after us. I was both proud and frightened for her.

We continued down the slope eventually completely out of sight of the tunnels or the highway. The small arms fire also stopped. We paused for a moment. After a few minutes we saw the transports lift off and fly away. We all took cover behind trees, rocks or bushes, but they all just flew away and out of sight.

"What do you suppose that's all about?" Peter asked.

"Nobody left to kill. Their job is done." Alex answered with his usual bluntness.

Then suddenly a tremendous explosion rocked the mountain. Smoke, rocks and dust were blown high into the air above us.

"Take cover!" I yelled.

Rocks came down all around us. Large boulders and chunks of concrete rolled past us. It was the trees and large granite outcroppings that protected us. And by God's grace, not one of us was hurt that day. But they had blown up the tunnels so that nobody could ever use them as a refuge again. None of us were in doubt that this long war had just begun.

CHAPTER 10

THE MARK

Three weeks had passed since we left what used to be Angel Camp. We descended into the lower elevations, living off the land in the foothills for several days until we came into the sparsely populated Inland Valleys. Time seemed to stand still for those areas far to the east of the city. I remembered them as sprawling suburbs, but most of the population had been moved out. The homes and businesses were neglected, abandoned and boarded up years ago.

The world was still at war as we were informed by a few Christians that we came across in hiding. They shared with us their meager provisions and the news that almost all of the believers who stood up openly against Anti-Christ were either dead, in prison or hiding out like us. Many Christians still were living in the cities and tried to keep their faith to themselves so that they might go on living reasonably normal lives. But most of us knew that wouldn't last long.

Anti-Christ was not only set on destroying believers, but all of his other political enemies as well. He was engaged in so many wars and conflicts around the world that no one could keep track of them all. But he seemed to be winning his wars and destroying his enemies by the millions with no end in sight. This preoccupation with conquest had stretched even his resources thin. Food was starting to be rationed. Fewer police were available to patrol the outlying areas to look for scavengers. There were plenty of empty buildings to hide in, but little food to be found.

We broke into an old empty house and held a meeting about how we should proceed.

"Friends, the time has come for us to look at our situation realistically. We are at war with a man, a government, a world that wants to exterminate us. They don't care much how they do it, whether they have to shoot us or starve us to death. There will be no negotiating with them and no defeating them. Therefore, we should try to survive by whatever means necessary apart from harming or stealing from fellow believers." I opened the discussion.

"Sounds like a plan to me." Alex weighed in.

"But then how are we different than them?" Eric Foster asked.

"Because they're evil and they're trying to kill us. It's just a question of self-defense, which is always justified." I answered back.

"Joshua's right. We're at war, and we will be until our Lord returns." Sarah added.

"I agree. I think we just take what we need from the bastards that are trying to kill us. But I also think we should help our brothers and sisters whenever we can." Peter's wife Amanda added.

Nods to the affirmative and words of agreement came from most of the group.

"Then I think we're all agreed that we take food and supplies from the establishment. But still we should keep a low profile and try not to be seen. And we kill only if there's no other choice." I tried to sum up and get a consensus.

I looked directly at Sarah, who turned out to be more of an aggressive fighter than I ever imagined.

"Agreed." Sarah said.

Then afterward everyone voiced their agreement.

There was a small Government run store in the old commercial district about two miles away. I proposed a plan whereby I would go there myself in the middle of the night after they closed, break in and take all the food and supplies that I could carry. But as Alex pointed out, I would most likely set off an alarm which would bring the police down on me in minutes. So it was decided that two of us would walk in during business hours with concealed handguns and conduct an old fashion hold up. We would tie up anyone who was in the store and hide them in a back room, preventing them from calling or sounding an alarm for a long time.

It was to be that Sarah and I would make the first foray into the world of crime. We were already criminals in the eyes of society simply by being followers of the Lord Jesus. But the whole order of right and wrong had been turned on its head in this world. All of us had determined to fight if necessary and survive if possible. Sarah gave Alex her automatic rifle and he gave her his handgun. We carried our weapons in our coat pockets. We also took some wool ski masks to cover our faces from the security cameras.

About noon the following day we set out from the house to the old commercial district. We walked about a hundred yards apart so that anyone watching us would not assume that we were together. The streets were unkempt and full of debris. There were few people or vehicles to be seen. Almost all of the homes and most of the businesses had been closed and boarded up for a long time. But a few businesses that were deemed necessary along with the people to run them were allowed to remain in the area. The Government established small convenience stores for people living and working in these outlying areas.

I stopped next to an abandoned building across the street from the store. Sarah came up and crossed the street, hiding by the building next to the store. Nobody could be seen outside the store, but we knew that surveillance cameras were inside and out.

We nodded to each other, and then we both put on our masks and made our move. The way was clear as we ran toward the automatic doors. When they opened, we both rushed in together, pulling our guns out. The store employee was a Latino man in his forties and he was talking to an older Asian man. Nobody else could be seen. We pointed our guns at them. They were both stunned by the sight of us.

"Hands on your heads! Don't move!" Sarah ordered.

They complied quickly as I secretly thanked God that they both understood English.

"Is there anyone else in the store?" I asked the attendant.

"No sir." He answered fearfully.

"I want you to open up these machines." I ordered.

Many of the goods that the store stocked including food were in what looked like large vending machines which were stacked side by side along the walls.

"I have to get the key. Over there." The scared attendant said as he pointed to a drawer behind the counter.

"Make it quick." I told him.

He walked over to the drawer and opened it slowly and carefully, trying not to spook me into shooting him. He pulled out the key which was just a simple plastic card that was inserted into a slot in each machine. When put in and withdrawn, the glass front would pop open. He went down the row of machines, opening up each one. Sarah held her weapon right in their face without saying a word. I could see that both men were scared, but I did not want to torment them unnecessarily.

"Now listen, if you both cooperate, nobody will get hurt." I told them.

I went behind the counter and grabbed a couple of rolls of packing tape as Sarah covered both men.

"Put your hands behind your back." I ordered the store attendant.

He did so without hesitation and I wrapped his hands together at the wrists with several layers of tape. I also put a couple of wraps around his mouth and then I walked him into the back room where I told him to get down on his knees. I lowered him gently down on the floor face down and then I taped his legs together.

"Just relax now; we're not going to hurt you." I tried to relieve some of his anxiety.

I went back up front and did the same to the Asian man, laying him on the same floor near the other. I felt that I had to reassure them both again that they would not be harmed. Then I heard Sarah yell to me.

"Hurry up!" She shouted.

We grabbed the biggest shopping bags they had and began stuffing them with food, bottled water, and anything useful we could find. Fortunately, nobody else had entered or approached the store. When our bags were full, we closed the glass doors on the vending units and ran out the door. When we got about a block away, we slowed to a brisk walk and removed the ski masks discarding them under the many trash piles we saw along the way. We again let some space develop between us as we walked, but always looking and listening.

By the grace of God we arrived back at the house safely where our friends were waiting for us. We had to carefully prop up the sheeting over the windows after we entered so it would not appear suspicious from the outside. Everyone was grateful for the bounty that we brought, but we all knew that we had to stay hidden in the house for several days. That night we could hear the distant roar of hoppers patrolling the neighborhood, no doubt looking for us. But after that first night they seemed to have abandoned the search.

The house was dark during the day because the openings were all boarded up. Only slivers of light penetrated through the seams of the sheeting. But at night, it was pitch black. You could not see your own hand in front of your face.

Sarah and I claimed one of the back bedrooms for our own. We actually enjoyed our stay in the abandoned house because the extreme darkness gave us a feeling of privacy again. I confided to Sarah that I didn't feel good about robbery, even if it was against the Government. She felt the same way. Neither of us pictured ourselves in this situation when we were growing up and learning right from wrong. But as she said many times, we were at war and war changes things. Food and supplies are weapons of war, so it's all fair game. I'm the one who was in the military and she never was, yet it turned out that she had more of the heart and mind of a warrior than I did. I told her that strong women turned me on and then proceeded to spend the next several hours proving it to her.

Jason was with our group and I considered him a friend. He brought with him only a fraction of his electronic equipment, but he did bring a portable satellite receiver. He tried to monitor news events for an hour or two each day. One day he picked up something that made our hearts sink, but was not unexpected. The "Prophet" unveiled several statues of Sheyer that were erected in major cities around the world. These statues were made to seem to come alive and speak. Now there were several technologies that existed which could accomplish that illusion. But everyone marveled at how real it all looked. The statues not only spoke, but could react and answer questions, all in Sheyer's own voice.

But the Prophet's plan did not stop there. He convinced those who were willing and ordered those who were not willing to bow down and worship at the feet of the statue. They were to thereby worship Sheyer by proxy. After the despicable event took place, they would be given Sheyer's mark either on their right hand or forehead. When the mark is applied, the person's DNA would be scanned into the world data base. Only those who had the mark could then buy or sell, pay or receive payment. This was going to be the way to ferret out the Christians who were secretly living among them. So not only would Christians be evicted from their homes, but they would be starved to death, and if caught, the penalty for refusal would be death.

It seemed that the more surreal things became, the less shocking they were to us because it was Biblical Prophecy being fulfilled word for word. Sheyer and the Prophet both knew that true Believers would never worship his image, so they created a whole world system designed to smoke out all Christians. There was no doubt; this was war to the end, war to the death.

As the days went on we stayed in the abandoned suburbs just trying to keep out of sight from the patrols. We found a different house or old office building to hold up in about every other night.

But while hiding, we were also moving slowly in a generally eastward direction. The police activity had increased ever since the Prophet's edict because many Christians, even whole families were trying to slip out of the city as I had done. Unfortunately, many of them were being intercepted before they got very far. We saw and even talked to a few who made it, and we gave them all the help we could. They told us of mass arrests and even people being shot down by police, including children.

One cold and overcast day Sarah, Alex and I were making our way back to the house where the others in our group were hiding out. We saw two police hoppers flying around our neighborhood. We took cover, but watched. They landed in the street close to the house. I don't know what had aroused their suspicion, perhaps one of the stealth drones got something on camera earlier. We hid ourselves behind the houses on the far end of the street. Both officers were out of their vehicles with weapons drawn.

"They're looking at the house." Sarah whispered.

"I think they're about to make their move. We've got to get around them, flank em." I answered.

"What do you mean?" Sarah asked.

"We've got to get behind them, sneak up on them from the back, from three sides and get them before they can get into the house." I told both Sarah and Alex as they listened intensely.

"What if Peter sees them and starts shooting?" Alex asked.

"We have to be in position before that happens. We'll go to each end of the street, behind the houses and work our way to the other side of the street. Sarah and I will go right, Alex you go left. Let's move!"

Sarah went first to place herself in the middle right behind the officers with her automatic rifle. I would cover their right side and Alex the left. We all moved quickly and quietly climbing over fences where necessary. It took a few minutes for us to get into position, but before we could, one of the officers used the PA speaker in his helmet to speak to the people in the house.

"This is the police. If anyone is inside the house, come out immediately with your hands on your head. This is your only warning."

Peter had no way of firing at them or even seeing them from inside because all of the doors and windows were boarded up. But he wisely kept silent. I didn't know if the officers were even certain that anyone was in the house.

But now all three of us were in position and moving toward the officers, with our weapons at the ready. One of them turned around and saw us, but before he could swing his weapon around, Sarah opened fire. We all opened fire and both officers were down in a few seconds.

Sarah moved quickly over to the dead officers while Alex and I met up behind her.

"I think Sarah got both of them." Alex remarked quietly to me.

"I wouldn't be surprised."

We quickly removed their helmets and kept them pointed away from us until we could bury them in some bushes on the side of the house. The helmets of course had built in cameras which constantly transmitted images back to headquarters. Alex pounded on the sheeting which covered the large front window and yelled to Peter and the others inside that it was all clear. One by one the others came out from the back of the house to gather with us in the front yard. Of course we took the officer's weapons and searched the hoppers for anything else we could find. But as I knelt down over one of the officers, I noticed a mark on his forehead.

"Look at that. Is that it? Is that the mark? I asked Sarah as I pointed to the dead officer's forehead.

"I think so." She said looking down at it curiously.

It was three short horizontal lines, one over the other and tattooed or branded in the center of the forehead. Upon closer look, the lines seemed to be made of miniscule small letters which I could not make out without magnification. Both officers had the same mark.

"I always thought it was going to be 666." I commented to Sarah.

"Well it must be in some form or another, I don't know. I'll have Jason look at it with his magnifying glass."

Meanwhile, we managed to open a locked compartment in one of the hoppers. It had more weapons and ammunition in it, including a very strange looking type of short assault rifle. The weapon's barrel had no opening in it; instead it was tipped by some kind of clear crystal. It also had no magazine or clip; in their place was some kind of a battery or power pack. When I turned back to look for Sarah, she was still standing over the dead officer and Jason was next to her with his magnifiers which he used for close electronic work. I could see that the young man was uncomfortable with the task.

"They're letters, laser printed letters burned into the skin." He said as he slid his viewer up to his forehead and looked back up at us.

"What do they read?" Sarah asked.

"Renard… Xer…X.E.R.X.E.S." Jason was having trouble pronouncing the middle name.

"ZERK-ZEEZ." I pronounced it for him.

"What kind of name is that?" Jason knew electronics inside and out, but he didn't concern himself much with history or culture.

"He was a king of ancient Persia. They called him the King of Kings and the King of the World." I explained.

"Renard Xerxes Sheyer, that's what the inscription, reads." Jason said as he looked back up at us.

"I wonder how you get 666 out of that?" I asked, just thinking out loud.

"Three names, six letters in each." Jason figured it out almost without hesitation.

"I hate to break up this discussion, but we've got to get the hell out of here!" Alex yelled to us as he and Peter were getting everybody ready to move out.

Of course Alex was right. It was almost certain that the police station was monitoring and had dispatched more officers or even soldiers to come after us. We picked up our things and ran down the street keeping close to buildings and staying mainly on the through streets. The pace we set had to be that of the slowest people in the group, but we had to stay together and we had to keep moving. The leaders kept looking back toward the western sky to see if police were coming.

We were surprised that we didn't see any hoppers or troop transports in the sky. After about an hour of running, we rested in an alley between two old commercial buildings. In the sector we were in, there were no operating shops or factories, no traffic in the streets and no other people to be seen. It was a true ghost town, but it was what most of the world looked like. After the collapse of financial systems and the natural disasters of a few decades ago, the world only rebuilt in the large cities where most of the population could be monitored and controlled.

During our rest stop, I took a closer look at the strange weapon that I was carrying. Some people had an opinion as to what it was, but Jason knew instantly.

"That's an Armatech 20 kilowatt laser rifle."

"A laser?"

"Yeah, they've been around for several years. They were banned and they stopped making them. They were considered an inhuman weapon."

"I can imagine. But apparently they're reconsidering that assessment. How do you operate it?"

"Well assuming that the power pack is charged, you push that back switch to the forward position. A green light should come on if the power pack has a charge and you can see on that little gauge how much energy you have left."

I did as Jason instructed and the little green light came on. The gauge registered almost a full charge on the power pack.

"Ok good. Now you see the three lit up buttons on the side, the ones with the symbols?"

"Yeah."

"The first is pulse, which means that the gun will fire only a short burst of energy each time the trigger is pulled. That's the setting used most often. The second is sustained. That's when you want the energy beam to continue for as long as you hold the trigger down, but that's only going to be about 90 seconds at full power. And the last button is your safety."

I took the weapon and readied it for firing. There was an old glass covered light high up on the outside wall of the next building. I took aim and fired a pulse. The glass exploded instantly and the fixture and concrete wall behind it were both charred black. Only a split second of a straight silvery white line of light could be seen coming from the barrel of the weapon. I was impressed and grateful that it was in our hands. As the others sat down and rested in the shade of the building, I kept the weapon and stood watch by the corner.

It wasn't twenty minutes later that I heard a buzzing sound in the sky. Suddenly three drones were hovering right over the alley entrance.

"Run!" I shouted.

But our group barely had time to get back on their feet before the first missile was fired. It overshot us by several feet, but the force of the explosion made a large hole in the outside wall and threw chunks of concrete in every direction, badly injuring a couple people. I took aim at the closest drone and fired a pulse. The drone exploded and caught fire in midair and soon crashed to the ground.

"Run for cover! Spread out! Scatter! Go!" I shouted.

We all ran out of the alley trying to confuse them with multiple fast moving targets. But the drones locked on to the closest target they could acquire. I rushed to the corner of the next building so I could turn and get another shot. There was another explosion in the street behind me. I turned back to see the bloody body of one of our group. It looked like a man, but I couldn't quite make out who it was. I aimed again and fired. The second drone was downed but not until after it took out one of our precious people.

The last drone was moving too fast. Sarah and the others were firing at it with conventional firearms, but with little affect. Then I heard another explosion behind some buildings about half a block away. I didn't see the result, but I knew I had to stop it. I ran after it down the middle of the street hoping that it would see me as a juicy target. It stopped and I stopped. I took quick aim and fired several rapid bursts. The last drone fell down to the street in fiery heap.

I heard our people crying over the dead and wounded. I looked around almost in a panic for Sarah until I saw her walking up the street towards me. She had tears in her eyes, but was otherwise in control.

"What's the damage?" I asked.

"Four dead, one badly wounded, one will recover." She reported with sadness.

"Dear God." I sighed.

"Joshua, Jason was one of those killed." She said as more tears flowed from her eyes.

My heart sunk within me. Jason had become my friend. He was a sweet, harmless young man. He couldn't fight or run fast and I guess he didn't know how to take cover. I thought over and over what would happen if I had been a little quicker, if I had taken the shot sooner. Sarah sunk her head into my shoulder. I held her close and we both started to cry. But we could only afford ourselves a brief moment of mourning. Eric's wife was critically injured in the alley and he would not leave her. We all understood and expected it. Her wounds were bandaged and she was made as comfortable as possible. But the rest of us had to move on.

There were no more attacks that day and our small group which was missing six beloved friends, managed to make another eight miles before sundown. We broke into a small commercial building which was very old. It may have been a store of some kind, but the interior was completely gutted. We all sat in a circle in the middle of the floor. After taking our restricted rations, Janet Chambers who just lost her husband earlier that day, began to pray and to praise God.

"Thank you Lord for your grace and mercy. You have redeemed us with your blood. We are yours. Who will we fear? Praise you Lord Jesus." She prayed out loud.

She inspired us all to not dwell on our trouble and loss, but to keep our thoughts on Him who saved us and who will return soon for us. We all slept peacefully that night in spite of what happened earlier that day. It was an incomprehensible sense of calm and even joy that filled our hearts. I would never have understood it before.

In the next several days, we made our way slowly eastward. There was no sighting of the enemy, but just as our food rations were running low, we came upon a closed and abandoned Government store. When we broke into it, we discovered that it had not been completely emptied. There was enough food and water to last us all several more days. We considered it a gift from God, but we did not stay there on the outside chance that it could be a trap. About three miles away we found the offices of a very large warehouse. It had carpeting and even a few pieces of office furniture left inside although it had been closed and abandoned for decades. Again, we all thanked God for His provision.

Sarah and I lay together on the floor that night just holding each other close.

"What are you thinking about?" She asked softly.

"I'm thinking about how much I love you."

"Why do you love me?"

"Because you're tough, you're smart, but you're good, and thoughtful and kind."

"I am?"

"Yes, plus you kiss good and you have a killer body."

She snickered and rubbed her face against mine.

"You think about that even now?"

"Honey, I'm a guy, we always think about it."

"Not just guys."

We kissed each other tenderly and held each other until we both drifted off to sleep.

The next morning was very strange indeed. There was complete silence from the outside world. Not a bird was chirping, not a breeze was blowing. When we emerged one by one from the building, we looked up and noticed an eerie reddish brown tint to the sky. It made the rising sun appear red while darkening and diffusing the light. Having grown up in Southern California, I recognized similar phenomenon when we would have brush fires or forest fires. The sky would be smoky brown for miles all around. But this was different. This was high in the upper atmosphere without any visible plume or clouds of smoke. If I could trace its origin, I would say that it was coming from the east, but from very far away.

We all stood outside the old warehouse just looking around, nobody saying a word. Then we saw a sight in the sky which both amazed us and terrified us. Suddenly a giant being appeared in the sky. It was hard to look at because it was so bright and striking. Its form and face was like a man's but very different. He wore a pure white tunic and over that were a bright gold breastplate and a golden sash around his waist. It was not a transparent image or projection. He appeared sharp and clear. His features were unmistakable even as he moved about and hovered in midair. When he looked down, it seemed that he was looking right at you and right through you, down into your soul. We were all frightened, but we could not move. We had to see what he was going to do. When he opened his mouth to speak, it was like the crack of thunder.

"Fear God and give Him glory, because the hour of His judgement has come. Worship Him who made the heavens, the earth, the sea and the springs of water."

He proclaimed the Gospel of Jesus Christ to the whole world and we knew that everyone in the world heard him and in their own language. It was an angel of God without any doubt and most of us thought that we would never see such a sight on this side of heaven. When he finished speaking, he disappeared and there was silence once again.

Some of our group dropped to their knees in prayer and worship to God. They praised God out loud with their eyes closed and their hands raised while the rest of us just looked at each other dumbfounded and waiting to see what would happen next. Soon after that, we saw a second angel appear in the sky. He also spoke in a loud voice to the whole world.

"Fallen! Fallen is Babylon the Great, which made all the nations drink the maddening wine of her adulteries." After he said this, he also disappeared.

We all were on our feet, silent and in awe, staring at the skies. And then a third angel appeared and delivered a loud message addressed to the whole world.

"If anyone worships the beast and his image and receives his mark on the forehead or on the hand, he too will drink of the wine of God's fury, which has been poured full strength into the cup of his wrath. He will be tormented with burning sulfur in the presence of the holy angels and of the Lamb. And the smoke of their torment rises for ever and ever. There is no rest day or night for those who worship the beast and his image, or for anyone who receives the mark of his name." After that, the third angel disappeared and the earth was silent.

None of us moved or spoke for almost an hour as we tried to assimilate all that we had just witnessed.

CHAPTER 11

A WORLD SHAKEN

The months that followed were a mixer of hardship, sadness and joy. Janet Chambers succumbed to an unknown illness, one which none of us had the ability to diagnose or treat. But she had very little pain; it was more like weakness overcame her and her body just shut down. I'll always remember her strong faith and her warm smile. Each of us held her hand near the end as we said good bye. We cried because we would miss her, but not because we felt bad for her. She told each one of us that we would all be reunited very soon. She died with a smile on her face and praising God. There was an old city park nearby. It was fenced off and overgrown with weeds. We buried her there in an unmarked grave, but God knew where she was.

We didn't see any more Government patrols for a while and for that we were grateful. The abominable proclamation and the subsequent warning of the angel prompted many to flee the cities and Government controlled areas. Unfortunately, most of the refugees would be civilians and many families, almost all of them unarmed. It would be easy pickings for the storm troopers to intercept them and either shoot them down or arrest them and take them to prison for God knows what fate. So I guess, the evil bastards were too busy rounding up defenseless Christians to bother with the few that made it to the outskirts, especially if some of them were able and willing to fight back.

Survival was an everyday task. Our rations were running low and we would supplement them by shooting some of the many crows which would circle around or perch on the rooftops in the late afternoon. Sometimes we bagged a stray coyote also. But even after cooking them thoroughly, we almost had to hold our breath while we ate because the smell and the taste were so rancid. They were good for sustaining life, but nothing else. Finding fresh water was also a challenge. It had not rained for a few months. When we found some standing water either in a flood channel or basin, we had to boil it and let it cool before we could drink it. Life was tough, but we were being toughened up to meet it. Yet we did not despair or lose hope. We laughed and sang and prayed together and comforted each other.

It was a very warm summer afternoon and the sun was still high in the sky, beating down on us relentlessly. We were on the move again. Some of us were trying to figure out exactly where we were. From a rooftop, we could see that we were in a very wide and flat valley with mountains to the north and a long range of high hills to the distant south. I guessed that we were somewhere around the old communities of Chino or Ontario, but there were no signs or indications left to tell me that, other than the estimated miles we have travelled and the familiar mountains to the north, which have not changed.

Suddenly, we heard a shout from up ahead.

"Stop, drop your weapons." A man's voice echoed through the concrete buildings.

Then we saw ten or twelve armed men emerge from around the buildings and on the rooftops. We found ourselves surrounded and some of us were ready to start shooting. They were not in any type of military or police uniform; in fact their clothes and appearance were rather grungy like us. I slowly set my weapon down on the reasonable probability that they were not with the Government. My companions one by one did the same.

"Hands on your heads, now!" The same man barked out the order as he walked up with his assault rifle trained on us.

We all promptly complied. The man was tall and husky. He appeared to be in his fifties and had long hair and a beard, both going grey. Sarah was in the lead so he approached her first. He examined her forehead very closely, which bothered me because I didn't know what he was going to do. He asked her to put out her hands, and then he examined them. Then he told her to go stand against the wall. It was the outside wall of a concrete building. I looked at Sarah as we were all getting increasingly nervous. As he was being backed up by his armed men, he repeated the process with each of us until all five of us were standing up against the wall looking at many weapons and angry faces lining up against us. I thought that maybe this was where we bought it. How could I have gotten it so wrong? It looked like I gambled and lost; now all of us would pay the price for my mistake. The man stood back as seven or eight of his men lifted their weapons and pointed them right at us.

"I'm sorry my love. Forgive me. I'll always love you." I said softly to my wife.

"I'll always love you, my husband." She said with a smile.

Then something unexpected happened. The man shouted out a strange question.

"Who is Lord?" He shouted and then paused for an answer.

We looked at each other not quite knowing what to make of it.

"Who is your Lord?" He demanded even louder.

"Jesus Christ is Lord!" We all shouted back almost in unison.

There was a stifling few seconds of silence where nobody moved or made a sound. Then, the armed men lowered their weapons. The leader smiled and extended his arms.

"Welcome, brothers and sisters. You have nothing to fear from us. We're sorry to put you through this, but we had to be sure."

He and his men approached us and extended their hand in friendship.

"I'm John Halloran. They call me Captain John, but you can just call me John."

We all shook his hand as we each introduced ourselves. Then one of his men walked up to him holding my laser rifle.

"Captain, look at this."

"A laser gun."

He took it and examined it with great interest.

"Who had this?"

"I did." I spoke up.

"Where on Earth did you get it?"

"God provides."

"Yes He does."

He turned and handed it to one of his men.

"Put this away with the others, and don't mess with it."

The man took the weapon and with the help of another soldier, they picked up all of our weapons off the ground and went out of sight around the building. Captain John turned back to speak to all of us.

"Don't worry; you'll all get your weapons back, except that laser rifle. I'd like to trade you something for it."

"What did you have in mind?" I asked.

"How about an Israeli-made titanium sniper rifle with scope and 100 rounds of ammo? It's about 40 years old but it's indestructible. It's a beautiful weapon."

I saw how much he wanted it, and I reasoned that they would put it to good use just as I did. There was also the fact we didn't have a lot of bargaining power from where we were standing.

"Sounds like a deal." I said with a sincere smile.

"That's great. Now you all will be our guest tonight. We'll give you a nice hot meal, a place to sleep and plenty of talk and fellowship. And when you leave in the morning, you'll take your weapons with maybe some extra ammo and all the water and rations you can carry. And if there's anything else I can do for you, just let me know."

"How about five pairs of new underwear?" I couldn't resist asking.

"What?"

"You scared the crap out of us back there."

He laughed out loud and then gave me a big bear hug which nearly squeezed the breath out of me. John was a strong man.

They took us to one of the large manual roll-up doors which was half way opened. We walked into a large warehouse with a cement floor and a ceiling about 40 feet high. Inside we could see several people milling around scattered crudely made structures. These were put together with shelving materials, crates and boxes from the old warehouse. The people made little homes for themselves inside the large building to give them a measure of privacy, which is something we didn't have much of at Angel Camp. The building was in much better shape than most of the commercial buildings that we passed by.

"How many people do you have here?" Amanda asked.

"Over 60 people live here, couples, families, even a few kids." John answered.

"How do you feed them all?" Sarah asked.

"We have a well-stocked supply store. It's not in this building, but it's nearby. Only a few of us access it. It's a secret, and we want to keep it that way. Not that we don't trust our people or you for that matter, but if anyone is ever captured, they can be made to talk."

The warehouse was lit only by the sunlight coming in through the open door. The air inside was cooler than outside, making it a great shelter for warm weather. The people looked at us out of curiosity but then soon went back about their business. I got the impression that they had seen and helped wandering Christians in the past. I asked John about that.

"We try to help as much as we can with food and temporary shelter, but the more people you have in one place, the harder it is for them to stay hidden. The Government is too busy right now to go out looking for a few scattered Christians, but they will come after a big group if they know about em."

"I know what you mean." I answered back while thinking of Angel Camp and Wrightwood.

"We're all mostly friendly people here, so say hello to somebody and I'll have Frank boil some water and get you some hot freeze-dried meals for supper. We have energy bars for desert and instant coffee."

"Thank you very much." Sarah said sincerely.

"You're all welcome. At around 21:00 most of us gather in the corner over there to hear a message or two and pray. But tonight I want to show you something that I think you need to see. Anyway, just make yourselves at home and I'll see you a little later."

We all thanked him as he turned and left us presumably to check on the armed watch or to collect some supplies from his secret store. The five of us stayed mostly together but we did strike up conversations with some of the people in the building. Most of them did not show or express any anxiety about their situation; instead they were grateful to have food, a place to sleep and just to be alive. I have become more and more astonished at the grace and peace that God gives His people even in these times. It really does surpass understanding.

The hot meals that we were served were just like home-cooked. I requested chicken and dumplings while Sarah enjoyed an Italian pasta dish. There was good food and conversation for a few hours. Then around nine o'clock people started gathering over to a far corner of the building where some makeshift benches had been set up. Not all of the people came however, some were standing watch, and some were just otherwise occupied. I also noticed that none of the children were present.

John was not only the head of security for the little community, but he appeared to be the spiritual leader as well. He led us all in a short prayer asking for the Lord's blessings and protection, but we also gave thanks for His provision and seeing us through this far. Then John opened something that looked like a small suitcase. It had a screen in the lid and a few controls below. He set the case down on a wood crate which was used as a table and then he turned the screen toward us.

"You all remember the Angels and what they said?"

We all nodded affirmative and said "Yes."

"The first Angel told the whole world that Jesus Christ is Lord and He alone should be worshipped. He said this in every language on Earth and to every person on Earth so nobody could ever say they were never told. The second Angel told us how Babylon the Great has fallen. For our guests who've been on the run for a while, several months ago New York City was levelled by a nuclear blast."

"From where? From who? I asked in shock.

"Nobody knows for sure, but Christians are being blamed."

"Do Christians have access to nuclear weapons?"

"No, of course not, but that doesn't matter. It was the big corporations who were funding the World Council and the World Bank from the beginning and most Believers knew this, so they made the connection that would further their hatred and war against us."

"That explains the red sky." Peter interjected.

"That's right. Tons of ultra-fine dust made its way into the upper atmosphere."

"Then who could have done it?" I continued to press to understand.

"Antichrist has lots of enemies, not just Christians. He's been able to pretty much conquer them all, but that doesn't mean that they all go away. Do you know that there's been food shortages and even starvation in many parts of the world? We hear that even in L.G. now a loaf of bread sells for 100 credits. But all those that refuse the mark have their World Bank account zeroed out and closed. They're not able to even buy food or anything else."

"What about Christians who are still in the city?" Amanda asked.

"I'm coming to that. The third Angel warned against worshipping the Beast or taking his mark. Well our brothers and sisters are not going to take the mark or worship the Antichrist. As you know, refusing to do so carries the penalty of death. But the death penalty is no longer being carried out by the traditional ways we all know, lethal injection or brain wave neutralization. Now they are going to make a public spectacle of it."

"Public spectacle?" I asked.

"I brought this to show you because otherwise, you wouldn't believe it. Last week we recorded a satellite feed broadcast of the public execution of Christians. 50,000 people packed into Montoya Stadium to witness and cheer the false Prophet's answer to the Angel's warning."

John switched on the video playback. The program opened up like a Super Bowl Game. Flashy titles and music opened the show as the cameras went close on an announcer who stood in the middle of the field. After the requisite homage to the Antichrist and false Prophet, the announcer turned the attention and the cameras to the sidelines. All around the perimeter of the field were wooden platforms that were shaped like crosses and set horizontally. Each platform had a person strapped down on it; face down with their head protruding over the top edge. My heart was racing, and all of our eyes were fixed on the screen. They showed close shots of the people on the platforms. They were men and women of all ages and races. There were children as young as ten and families strapped down beside each other. Some of the people were singing, some were praying, some were crying. Children and teenagers were crying and yelling to their mothers or fathers and many more just silently lay there awaiting their fate. I could not help but to think of the Jensens. Could they be among those on the field?

Throughout all eternity I'll never forget what we witnessed next. A line of people walked out to the field wearing red jumpsuits. They walked over to a large rack which had swords stacked up on it, each in its own holder. One by one they each grabbed a sword and walked up to stand over a waiting victim.

There were about 60 people carrying swords and about 600 people lying on the crosses. John told us that 600 people won a lottery to participate in the event. Ten groups of 60 would eventually come out on the field. The first group stood by ready until the command was given over the loudspeaker, "raise your swords". They raised their swords over their heads. A few seemed singularly uncoordinated. Then came the command, "strike". The shiny steel blades came down as human heads rolled out onto the field and blood poured out like an open drain pipe. Some of the killers missed the victim's neck altogether and hit the scull or the back. Some had to take two or three strokes to finish the job. After the gory deed was done, the killers would raise their swords to the crowd who went wild with cheers and applause.

We all cringed in disbelief as we watched. These were citizens of the State who asked for and were given a license to commit murder and being cheered on by other citizens. As the first group exited the field, another group followed also wearing red jumpsuits. The camera was not shy about showing the decapitated bodies and the bloody heads on the ground. The people on the crosses were screaming and yelling. When the camera got close to a young girl screaming and crying out to her mother, I saw my own daughter, I saw the Jensen's daughter in her. I had to turn away as the blades came down. I couldn't take it anymore. I got up and walked over to the far wall. I think that the rest of my group had enough as well, they turned off the video but only Sarah followed after me.

"Are you alright darling?" She said softly, putting her hand on my shoulder.

"I'm so angry; I can't see straight, I can't think straight. I just want to kill, kill them all."

"I know, but God can do what you and I can't. He'll judge and punish them perfectly and completely. We have to leave it in His hands."

"It was like they weren't even human. They made a sport out of killing them." I grumbled on not being able to get the images out of my mind.

"Let's go back." Sarah said as she pulled me gently back over to the group.

"I'm sorry everyone, I just lost it for a moment." I apologized to the group.

"I think we all feel the same way." Amanda said.

"I'm sorry, I sure didn't mean to upset all of you, but this is real, it's actually happening to our brothers and sisters. Consider yourselves blessed because so far, you're out of the hands of the Government. Keep it that way. Never surrender to them. If you have a choice, die fighting." John lectured us.

"You better know it." Alex answered defiantly.

After the meeting broke up, Sarah and I made our bed on the spacious concrete floor. The small personal lights dimly lit the roof trusses high above. I stared for hours at the ghostly framework, not really seeing it, but still thinking about those video images. After an unknown amount of time, I fell asleep.

It was a sunny, dry and cloudless summer morning. The temperature at 8:00 AM gave us every indication that it was going to be a hot day. We enjoyed a delicious breakfast of instant eggs, instant pancakes and instant coffee. When we assembled outside, John and some of his people were busy loading us up with water and food rations. True to his word, he returned our weapons, with a little extra ammo thrown in and he handed me a very nice sniper rifle with 100 rounds of ammo in exchange for my laser rifle. John also handed me a long machete in a hard canvas sheath. He told me that it was for cutting through thick brush if we had to suddenly flee into the hills. I strapped it to my belt.

"We want to thank you all for everything." I said to John and company.

"We're family." John answered back.

"Do you have any suggestions as to where we should go? I asked.

"If I were you, I would head south, toward the hills. You should find water along the way and you can cross under the Strategic Highway if you need to through one of several drainage channels."

"Strategic Highway?"

"Yeah, it was one of the old Interstate Highways, one of the few that are still open, but it's all walled up on each side with razor wire and cameras on the wall. Stay well away from it during the day so the security cameras won't spot you."

"What's up in those hills?" Peter asked.

"Oh, it's nice up there. There's forests, streams; some deer and other game, at least there were years ago when I was up there last. There were even the remains of a little town. The road's been long closed to vehicles but you can walk up. I'm sure you're used to that."

"Yeah, I guess we are." Peter answered back.

We shook hands and said our final goodbyes and then set out on an industrial side street. As before we tried to stay as close to buildings and other cover as we could. In two days we came to the Strategic Highway. It was as John described, covered by high walls on each side. Nobody could tell how many vehicles if any were on it. We kept it in sight from a distance as we paralleled the highway in a generally southward direction.

After several more days, we found ourselves in an increasingly rural setting. There were the ghosts of once sprawling suburbs scattered amongst farms and vast empty fields which lay fallow. The trees and the grass were still mostly green and alive, but all those things built long ago by man seem to be dead and rotting. We all could see from time to time, distant figures hiding and skulking about, some just standing in the distance observing us. It comforted us to believe that these were Christians like ourselves who managed to escape the clutches of the Government. They were probably people who desperately tried to survive as we did, but most likely with few or no weapons. They were not likely to reach out to us, for either they stay hidden, or they risk capture and certain death.

More long, warm days and nights passed as we made our way south to the towering green range of hills. We found water in old flood channels and a river which was reduced to no more than a stream because of the draught. If the water was flowing and did not smell bad, then we would just add a couple of chlorine drops to it. But if it was stagnated water, we would boil it for 15 minutes and let it cool. There were an abundance of rabbits in the area as well as possums and raccoons. We managed to bag several of these in our travels which helped our rations to last longer. And because it was still warm, we slept outside beneath clumps of trees with one of us awake and on watch at all times.

We came to a respectable size city in which the housing projects would back right up against the hills. Going through the remains of the town we passed many houses long condemned but we knew that people were taking shelter in them as we had done. At that point, we no longer feared Government troopers or drones. We walked the streets openly in the light of day. I think that we came to a point where we preferred a fight and possible death rather than forever lurching in and out of the shadows. But obviously the denizens of the city did not feel the same way. They kept to themselves and kept hidden. They would not seek help or confront strangers. We knew that they were mostly Christians. What else would they be? Still, we felt sorry for them, but they would not show themselves openly and there was little we could have done to help them. We kept on walking.

By afternoon we reached the outskirts of town by the base of the green, tree laden hills. Suddenly, Alex who was walking point held out his arms to stop us.

"Hold it."

"What is it?" Sarah asked.

"Look over there by that house. What are those things?" Alex pointed to a solitary house surrounded by woods on three sides.

We all looked hard at the three bullet shaped objects parked in front of the distant house.

"They're hoppers!" I finally recognized them, especially after noticing an officer standing by them.

"How can you tell from here? They're not white." Peter complained, not being able to see distances sharply.

"They've been painted green and brown, but they're hoppers. There's an officer out there too." I insisted.

"Well then we better get out of here before they spot us." Amanda said nervously.

"You got that right." Peter agreed.

The couple started to take off on a 90 degree tangent to the left.

"Wait!" I shouted.

They stopped in their tracks and came back.

"Wait for what?" Peter asked anxiously.

"They're not here on vacation. They're looking for Christians."

"We know that."

"Well, it looks like they found some."

"What do you expect us to do about it?"

"Help if we can. You all remember the video. You know what they do to our brothers and sisters. We can't just walk away." Sarah drove home her point with conviction.

Peter thought about it and then looked remorseful.

"You're right. I'm sorry. They need us. I'm not a coward."

"Of course you're not brother. If they were after us, the right thing to do would be to run and hide. But now, we have the chance to sneak up on them and take em by surprise."

"What's the plan?" Alex looked at me and asked.

"There's an officer outside. He's not wearing his helmet. You go in first, but don't shoot, just cover him. Amanda will stay outside and cover the house. Then Peter, Sarah and me will rush into the house. Okay?" I explained to Alex while everyone else listened closely.

There was little cover between us and the house, so we separated and made a wide swing through the woods. Sarah, Peter and Amanda went to the left, Alex and I went to the right. We crept slowly and kept behind cover as we approached the house from two sides. As we got closer, we could hear the sounds of loud talking and some screaming, women screaming from inside the house. A single officer was standing outside leaning up against one of the hoppers. Alex snuck up through the trees as close to the clearing as he could get. When the officer turned to watch the house, Alex made his move. He pulled out his pistol and pointed it at the officer while walking quickly up behind him. The officer heard him coming and turned around.

"Don't move, don't make a sound or you're dead. Hands on top of your head. Get down on your knees." Alex ordered in his meanest tough guy tone.

The officer slowly complied but it looked like his mind was racing to figure a way out.

"Please, just give me one little excuse to blow your head off. How many officers in the house?"

"Two."

Alex lifted up his free hand and held up two fingers without taking his eyes off his prisoner for even a second. The rest of us rushed in toward the house. When we got there, we saw a man lying face up in the front yard. He had been shot several times including twice in the head rendering him all but unrecognizable. There was no time for grief as the screams continued from inside. We gathered at the front door which was partially open. Sarah switched her assault rifle to full auto and went in first. Peter followed close behind her with his automatic pistol. I covered them both with my weapon.

Almost instantly I heard Sarah open fire. I rushed in. It's hard to describe what I saw. Two half-dressed officers were standing over two women who were stripped naked and tied face down onto two beds which were moved next to each other. One of the officers reached for his weapon on the floor, but Sarah riddled him with bullets from his head to his groin before he could reach it. The other officer could not reach his weapon so he threw his hands up in surrender. As I looked at the two women screaming and crying, I quickly put some assumptions together in my mind. The women were a mother and her teenage daughter. The dead man outside was the husband and father. My blood boiled and I saw and heard only as if through a narrow tunnel of hate.

Sarah and Peter were about to shoot him, but I stopped them. I walked up to him pointing my rifle at him, and then I turned it around and rammed the stock into his solar plexus. He doubled over in pain. I grabbed the back of his shirt collar, cutting off his air as I dragged him through the length of the house to the front door.

"Joshua! What are you going to do?" Sarah demanded.

"Go take care of the women." I yelled back.

I pulled him out of the house and dragged him into the front yard with strength I never knew I had. Amanda came up to me.

"What's happening?"

"Go inside and help Sarah."

Peter followed me out but Amanda still stood there trying to figure out the situation.

"Mandy, there're two women in the house, they need your help. Go on." Peter said to his wife.

I dragged the officer over to within sight of the other one. He was on his hands and knees in agony and gasping for breath. I then called out to Alex's prisoner.

"Hey you, tough guy, I thought you could use some entertainment." I said in a maniacal tone.

I then pulled my machete out of its sheath.

"Josh!" Peter yelled to me.

"Doesn't it amuse you to see heads cut off? I know how hard you all work for Satan, so I thought I would bring you a little entertainment, watch."

The officer was looking down as I raised the machete. At the last moment he looked up at me as I brought the blade down on his neck as hard as I could. It was a quick, clean sever. His head rolled a couple of feet and I saw his eyes flutter and then go blank. The body collapsed in a pool of blood. I dropped the machete and stood there as if in a nightmare waiting for it to end.

"That guy's crazy!" The other officer yelled at Alex.

"You guys have that effect on some people." Alex answered back.

"What are you going to do with me?"

"I'm glad you asked that."

Alex then fired point blank into his forehead. The officer fell back, dead.

Sarah rushed out of the house.

"What's going on out here? Oh, my God!"

"I'm sorry; I lost control for a while."

"You think?

I couldn't speak even to apologize any more. I walked over to the trees. Sarah followed.

"Darling, don't let hate eat you up. It's not about them, it's about you. You're the one I care about. We need you. I need you."

"How are the women?"

"They'll be all right. We should stay with them for a couple of days."

"Whatever you say, my love."

We embraced each other which brought me back from the bad place I was in.

CHAPTER 12

THE DARKNESS AND THE LIGHT

The family's name was Martinez. The wife Annabel recovered remarkably quickly from the horrific ordeal. Her 15 year old daughter Debra was going to take a lot more time. She spoke very little and we could see that the physical and emotional scars would take their toll on her. We buried Greg Martinez on the property with all the dignity that was in our power. As for the three renegade officers, we dragged their bodies deep into the woods for the scavengers and insects to take care of. We found more weapons and rations in the hoppers. My idea was to use the hoppers to transport us to the back side of the steep hills.

It was the morning of the third day and we were about to depart when Alex came up to us with an uncharacteristic emotional appeal.

"Guys, I've been giving it a lot of thought. I want to stay here. Annabel and the girl need someone now more than ever."

"What do they say?" I asked.

Alex called over to Annabel who was standing by the house. As she approached him, he extended his arm to her and she moved into it, embracing him. This definitely was not a part of Alex that I have ever seen.

"It's been eating at me for years. You've got Sarah, Pete's got Amanda. I just don't want to be alone anymore. I want someone to love, and someone to love me. You understand, don't you?"

"Yes, I do. Annabel, you're getting a good man, I promise you that."

We conducted one of the shortest wedding ceremonies and adoption proceedings in history. Peter presided and in the presence of God and all of us, Alex and Annabel committed themselves to each other and Alex also agreed to protect and provide for Debra as his own daughter. We left the new family with weapons, rations and one of the hoppers. I instructed Peter and Alex on the operation of the hopper. Basically, if you set it to FLY AUTO then you could not crash, unless you ran out of fuel. After embracing our old friend and our new ones, the four of us took off ascending the steep slopes to the high summits.

Peter lagged behind because he was afraid to let it open, but it was understandable since he had never been in a hopper before. I think Sarah was surprised and impressed on how well I handled one. I actually came to enjoy flying them.

The hills were covered in green trees and vegetation, but the back slopes were too steep to land a hopper, much less as a place to settle. We continued to fly south until we spotted a large murky pond that looked as if it used to be a sizeable lake at one time. There was the remnant of an old highway which went from the lake, up to the summit of the hill and beyond. The summit was relatively flat and covered by a beautiful forest of live oak and other trees. Looking down through the trees, we could see structures, like a little town or village. We also saw streams which seemed to run alongside the highway in many of the steep canyons.

The hoppers were undoubtedly equipped with some sort of hidden transponder or homing device. So we had to ditch them in an area away from where we were going to be. There was a clearing on the front slope, overlooking the lake and the old town. We landed on the clearing and pushed the vehicles over the side resulting in both erupting in a fiery explosion.

The road was intermittently broken by rocks and dirt covering it from old landslides. In some cases we had a steep climb up the side of the hill to get up and around some of the larger slides. Both women made me proud to see their skill and stamina in climbing the steep and rugged hillside. Pete and I were struggling just to keep up. After about two hours, the road leveled out, we had reached the summit. There were distant scenic views behind us and a green forest ahead of us.

As we moved slowly forward, it looked like we were entering a parkland or campground, which it probably was at one time. We could see some structures scattered through the woods. They appeared to be well maintained, not abandoned or vandalized like so many others we had seen. But then we were all taken by surprise.

"Stop right there! Put your weapons down, get your hands up and walk forward, slow." The man's voice came out of nowhere at first until suddenly we saw him and about a dozen other armed men approach us from both sides of the road.

We complied because they were not Government officers. They were common people, most likely Christians just protecting themselves as we had seen before, as we had done. Their weapons were not military style, but very old home defense or sporting weapons that citizens once possessed. The men circled us as the leader came forward.

"Who are you?" He asked while pointing his pump action shotgun toward us.

"We're Christians seeking asylum with other Christians." I answered boldly.

"Is the Government after you?"

"They're after all of us."

"Just earlier today, we saw a couple of hoppers buzzin around here. Were they looking for you?"

"That was us." Peter answered.

"What do you mean that was you?"

"We mean that we're no strangers to fighting. We found some officers attacking a Christian family several miles back. We killed the officers and took their hoppers and then we dumped the hoppers off the side of the hill and walked the rest of the way up. I continued the story.

The man lowered his weapon and looked at us with intense thoughtfulness.

"You can put your hands down."

"We offer you the weapons that we brought with us and our rations to be used by your people; we only ask that you take us in. We're tired of running."

A couple of the men picked up our weapons and brought them up to show the others.

"Look Jake, these are good weapons, we don't have anything like em in camp."

"And we know how to use them. I promise you that we will defend you; we'll work hard and pull our weight. We offer friendship and fellowship. Please, all that we ask is that you give us a place to rest and to wait for the coming of our Lord."

Jake extended his hand of friendship to us as did the others and they welcomed us into their community. God has given us another short respite in the midst of the storm.

The four of us were given a small, two bedroom cabin that needed some work to become habitable. It had been used for supply storage, but we worked hard to make it a home. Life in the Camp was far more bearable than being on the run. The Camp itself contained about 300 people but a portion of that number was made up of people who had lived in the remote village for decades. We easily integrated ourselves amongst the loving Believers there. There was always hard work and vigilance required for almost everyone. This camp was less military oriented than some Christian camps, but Jake and some of the other leaders did appreciate our weapons and our fighting experience. We all did work hard, but we also took time out for relaxation with visiting neighbors, card games, board games and Bible studies. There was a young man a techy nerd named Ben in the camp. He was of East Indian decent, but his habits and mannerisms reminded me of Jason. As with Jason, we made friends quickly. He could build or repair devices that could monitor World Net broadcasts and he even kept the old gasoline generators running when they were needed. We found ourselves in relative peace in the months that followed, but never forgetting those we left behind.

The broadcasts of Christian executions were still coming in from around the world. Ben monitored and reported on them, but nobody had the heart to watch them. We were all reading the Book of Revelation and other end time prophesies in the Bible. It was the topic of conversation among friends, family and Bible studies. The idea was to use the Scriptures as a blueprint to see what had already happened, what was happening and what was to follow. It was uncanny to see the events being fulfilled so accurately, and in the proper sequence. The exact time of any event could not be predicted, but as the months rolled on and we calculated about three and a half years since Anti-Christ was given power, we all waited for the other shoe to drop.

It was a cool spring evening when Ben called a meeting for anyone who was willing or able to attend. The largest building in the camp was the old fire station which was used as a dormitory for about 40 people. But that night, about 150 people crowded in to see and hear a special broadcast on Ben's portable receiver.

A Special Report from Jerusalem at the site of the Great Temple brought thousands of adoring spectators and media from all over the world to witness what was being called the greatest event in history. Sheyer, who we call the Anti-Christ and the Cardinal, who we call the False Prophet stood together just outside of the entrance to the magnificent temple. The building itself was not enormous but so impressive in its construction. It was a rectangular structure, almost 100 feet long, about 30 feet wide and over 40 feet high. The outer walls were made from a light colored polished stone with smaller out buildings against the walls of the main temple. There were stone steps which led from the inner court to the wide open portico which was framed in by a grand pillar on each side. Even from the outside, everyone could see that the complete interior walls, floor, ceiling and carvings were covered in real gold leaf and gold foil, reflecting its bright yellow radiance to the outside of the building.

The following spectacle was staged for the most dramatic effect. The Anti-Christ stood at the very entrance of the Temple. He was dressed like an ancient king, wearing a white tunic, covered by a purple robe and having a gold crown on his head with ten spires. The False Prophet was standing in front about three steps down. He was dressed as an ancient prophet, or at least as the popular perception of one. On each side of the steps stood twelve men and women dressed to resemble priests. They were handpicked devotees while the regular Jewish Temple Priests were conspicuously absent. The False Prophet began to address the gatherers.

"People of the world, today we come to proclaim a new order and a new kingdom on Earth. The old sacrifices and oblations are hereby abolished because they are no longer necessary. All of the old divisions and strife among the world's religions have now passed away. For our Leader is the culmination and fulfillment of all the world's religions, of all of their prophesies and of all their ultimate purposes. He is the one for whom the whole world has waited. He alone has shown that he has the power to unite the world, and he alone has shown himself to be god above all else that is called god. Come, let us worship him now."

The Anti-Christ then turned and entered the Temple, followed by the False Prophet and the 24 so-called priests. The cameras followed them into the massive golden chamber. The Anti-Christ stood in the middle of the chamber as his priests and the False Prophet dropped to their knees and bowed their heads down to worship him. He stood there boldly and stretched out his arms.

"I am your one and only god. Serve me and live in peace, unity and joy."

I looked over at Sarah who was standing next to me. She was riveted by the proceedings, mostly with disbelief and anger. Her eyes were full of rage as her Jewish blood boiled within her. She didn't want to turn away, rather she wanted to jump through the screen and cut his throat. When we all had enough, Ben turned it off and we dispersed back to our own quarters.

Through our study of scripture, we knew that the forces of Anti-Christ had already overrun Jerusalem and the land of Israel, or they would do so shortly. This was exactly the time in which Jesus warned believers to flee immediately. The Bible also taught that the Jews would find temporary refuge in the old Kingdom of Jordan, while God unleashed his wrath on the minions of Anti-Christ. The two indestructible Witnesses in Jerusalem, who had the power to bring plagues and death to the mindless followers of this diabolical leader, and the 144,000 righteous men of Israel who would be sealed and protected from the terrible plagues to come, were signs by God that the land of Israel would never again be completely occupied by gentiles.

There on our quiet hilltop the Lord had sustained us. We had rain over our local terrain so that the stream had water in it. Wild game, even deer were taken out of the forest to sustain us. But in the days and weeks following the desecration of the Temple, we noticed bizarre signs from the sky and on the Earth. We saw dark clouds which looked like they were pouring hard rain and hail in the distance. But then the hills or towns would erupt in flames below it. We saw the landscape dotted with fires and even great forest fires and brush fires spread out in various spots across the horizon. If a fire rushed through these canyons, we would have been devastated, but thank God, no fire came near us.

Everyone seemed more sober and introspective as we all waited and anticipated the coming of the Lord. There was less of an appetite to indulge in carnal pleasures, even lawful ones. Sarah and I found ourselves just holding each other quietly through the nights. Even so, our love for each other grew daily. It was more of a spiritual connection than a physical one. As often happens with couples who have been together for many years, they learn to love the soul of the other person. God was refining our marriage in the short time that we had together.

I was standing watch alone one night on the summit. There was a cool breeze blowing. The stars were out and the fires had subsided. Suddenly, a bright light flashed in the western sky. I thought at first that it was lightning, but I could see a bright fiery object falling from the sky. It did not just vanish like a falling star but it fell all the way down and then the whole sky lit up for a split second like daylight. It took about three seconds for the sky to dim from bright white to yellow to orange and then dark again.

Then I heard the most frightening, low pitched, sustained thunder imaginable. The thunder was loud and shook the whole world. I jumped off the rock I was standing on before I was knocked down the side of the hill. It was one of the most startling things that I've experienced in months. My guess was that a giant asteroid had hit the Earth hundreds of miles west of us and landed in the Pacific Ocean. The flash and shockwave startled the whole camp. I was probably the only one in camp to see the whole thing. I offered my opinion as to what it was. Jake believed that it was one of the Trumpet Judgements from the book of Revelation. I would not at all be surprised if it was.

In the days to follow, there appeared strange signs in the heavens. These must have been terrifying to the world, but to Believers in hiding, they were a welcome relief because the pressure was being taken off the persecuted and poured onto the persecutors. It was late afternoon and I had returned with the foraging party when suddenly, the sky was ablaze with the biggest fireworks display the world has ever seen. Another asteroid hit the atmosphere with a blinding light somewhere far to the northeast. It broke up into thousands of smaller pieces that were cascading downward like white hot flares and then they burned up and faded away. That asteroid I would surmise probably rained down billions of tons of cosmic dust and particles over at least one third of the Earth's surface.

The fine dust which remained in the upper atmosphere soon

spread to cover the whole planet. The effect of the dust covering was that the light of the sun by day and the moon by night were diminished by a third. If the sun or moon could be seen through it, they appeared blood red. And if any normal clouds formed under the dust canopy, the midday light would be no greater than twilight. And so we remained under a cover of darkness which gradually grew darker as time went on.

There was a concern among Ben and the more scientifically trained people in camp that the next several rains may contaminate the streams. That was a possibility that I hadn't thought of, but they were probably right. We topped off every tank, barrel and jar with fresh water before the rains came again. But up to that point, we had not been harmed by the calamities that were coming upon the Earth.

Satellite reception became intermittent. But when we did get a signal, we saw signs of death and devastation around the world in spite of the Government censors effort to minimize it. It seemed that a great plague had broken out in Europe and spread to various parts of the world. It sounded similar to the Bubonic Plague that wiped out half of the population of Europe almost a millennium ago. In addition to that, it was reported that holes would appear randomly in the dust canopy and when that happened during the heat of the day, it would somehow magnify the intensity of the sun's rays and inflict second degree burns on anyone caught out in it. But no plague or calamity affected our camp or our people.

We all became accustomed to the darkness for it became our new reality. Most of us memorized every tree and every rock and every building and knew how many paces there were between them. So we tried to keep the use of lights outside to a minimum. We had not seen any recent signs of the enemy, but from what we could glean from the final transmissions, they had been thinned out pretty well. But still, the ones that remained were full of anger and vengeance, not only against God's people, but against God Himself.

As in any war, boredom and complacency takes over after weeks and months pass by without seeing action. At some point we had given up posting security watches. I guess people thought that they were no longer needed and the Lord was going to return at any time. Sarah, me and a few others kept our weapons close at hand, but most of the camp was eagerly anticipating the coming of the Lord. They would spend most of the day in prayer, both individually and in groups. They were singing and rejoicing like besieged soldiers seeing reinforcements riding to their rescue.

It was another quiet day as Sarah and I attended a Bible study and worship service in the old Ranger Station. We were immersed in it mentally and emotionally until suddenly we heard a sound in the distance that we recognized all too well. It was the jet roar of a military troop transport. Everyone was silent.

"Get your weapons and take cover in the woods!" I shouted as Sarah and I reached for our weapons which were leaning up against the back wall.

Some of the people were screaming and shouting as they tried to all rush out of the two doors. Then I heard gunshots but I could not see any soldiers. Bright lights were shining through the trees and people were running back and forth in frenzy. I heard automatic weapons firing and I could see some of our people fall. Sarah and I retreated into the woods, taking cover tree by tree as we looked for a target. The shooting and the killing went on and I feared that our people were getting the worst of it. Then four troopers appeared out of the shadows. Sarah and I opened up on them. She got two of them with her automatic rifle. I got one with my sniper rifle and the other one took cover.

"Get back, I'll cover you!" Sarah shouted at me just before she opened up on the advancing troops.

"Come on Sarah, run!" I shouted.

I was looking for a target of any trooper that would pop his head out long enough for me to get a shot. Sarah had them pinned down but then she stopped firing. She had run out of ammunition.

"Sarah, come on!" I shouted as I tried to cover her with my single shot rifle.

Then three troopers ran toward us with guns blazing. I hit the middle one in the face, but out of the corner of my eye, I saw Sarah fall face down to the ground. She didn't move.

"Sarah!" I cried.

The two other troopers ran fast after me as bullets flew all around me. I turned and fired and thought I saw one of them fall. I then tried to run deeper into the woods when I suddenly felt a burning pain in my side. I dropped my gun and ran to the edge of the hill where I tumbled over the side. I slid down the slope until a large bush broke my fall.

Many times in life we think about how our end will come, and when it does come all we have to say is "so this is it?" Sometimes we don't have time to reflect on it, Sarah didn't. Oh, my dear Sarah, I love you. Now I lay here on this hillside waiting to die, looking out into a dark but open sky. As I lay there with my hand over the bleeding wound, I felt at peace and grateful. I was grateful that the pain was bearable and I was grateful that I had a chance to reflect over my long journey which was coming to an end. I realized that God had guided me on my journey all along and through it, I found what I was seeking, I found purpose, I found love and I found the Lord.

I closed my eyes and put my head back as I prepared for death. But death did not come. I lingered there on the hillside, unable to move and unable to die. The sounds of battle from above were all silent. Sarah, my friends, everyone in camp was probably dead. But are they dead? No, they're alive, never to see death again.

It was a dark day, but it was day and still I held on. The bleeding had slowed to a trickle as it dried and caked around my hand. I was weak, but still conscious and I wondered why I could not just go to sleep. I gazed at the sky.

Then I heard the sound of trumpet that was so loud that it vibrated the hills. Immediately after that were loud voices from the sky shouting: "The kingdom of the world has become the kingdom of our Lord and of His Christ, and He will reign forever and ever."

Even before they finished speaking, I saw the sky open up with blinding light from horizon to horizon. And I saw millions of people, all in bright white robes descending in bright clouds behind the Lord

Jesus Himself. But as soon as I saw this, I instantly became a part of it. I was in the air; the Lord looked at me and smiled. I saw Sarah. I saw Kathy and Audrey. I saw the Jensens and all of my friends. We were all changed and descending to Earth with a purpose.

Jesus rode a white horse and wore a blood red robe. I could see the armies of Heaven following behind him and He had sharp sword. There are no adequate words to describe my present state. I have no more pain and no more fear. No more fear for me or those I love. I no longer struggle with temptation or weakness. I am strong, and will be forever. I am happy and fulfilled in every way. I am alive.

www.ingramcontent.com/pod-product-compliance
Lightning Source LLC
Chambersburg PA
CBHW021552310726
48972CB00003B/788